DEMON HUNTED

First edition. September 13, 2025.

Copyright © 2025 Ysadora Sonderling.

ISBN: 978-1763687455

Written by Ysadora Sonderling.

To my readers, your support keeps me going.

To OneDrive, for making me lose all of my edits multiple times. I uninstalled you and have the last laugh.

DEMON HUNTED

By

Ysadora Sonderling

Sonderling
Publishing House

Chapter One

'Well, that was a barrel of laughs,' Tessa quipped, tired and bloody after working another night-time patrol of downtown Bayton. She automatically switched the kettle on and set out two badly chipped mugs. Lee settled himself on the couch in his usual fashion, draping his muscular body across its length like some kind of couture fashion model. It was a grace that belied his massive frame and rather impressive horns protruding from his head. He simply shrugged in response, letting Tessa vent after another hard night's work. Despite needing to keep Lee hidden from the Agency, lest he be banished immediately, he still accompanied Tessa on her night patrols. There was no way she was risking the back alleys of Bayton without some extra protection.

'I am so sick of these patrols! I mean really, busting poor street kids or sex workers for using delusion and sex spells is not what I saw myself doing with my life!' Tessa exclaimed as she poured the tea and carried both cups to the lounge room. Lee simply nodded, knowing there would be no need for a response when she was in such a mood.

Tessa just needed to let off steam, huffing her way around the house. She slurped her tea loudly while scrubbing various parts of the kitchen, anger cleaning away the night. Even though she was exhausted, Tessa attacked the grime in her kitchen with gusto.

When she had drenched and scrubbed every cupboard door she finally calmed down. Stalking back into the lounge, Tessa threw herself on the couch beside Lee with a loud huff.

'You're just pissed because that blonde one clawed your face. I'm sorry I didn't have time to stop it. I am sure the Agency will have some kind of disgusting murder ready for you soon enough. Then I will have to listen to you whine about that all day.' Lee laughed as Tessa pretended to look insulted.

'Oh really?' she jokingly snapped before she launched herself at him, tickling all the places he hated most. They wrestled energetically until suddenly a loud crack ceased their actions and they found themselves on the floor in a pile of splintered wood and perished couch stuffing. The weathered old couch had finally given way.

'Oh no! My beautiful couch, do you know how long I have had this?' Tessa asked, in mock annoyance.

'By the looks of it, probably since the last witch's council,' Lee laughed, pulling himself and Tessa out of the debris. The couch had indeed been utterly destroyed, only the arms stood unbroken. They bravely stood alone like residual monuments to what was once her gloriously ugly couch. The rest was a mass of perished foam and brown velour. Here and there shards of wood stuck out. Tessa looked to Lee with a pained grin on her face.

'Guess it's time to go furniture shopping. I really need a new case soon as possible. The bonus from the last one is almost used up buying you a damn wardrobe and all that pomade. Seriously, who needs that much pomade?' she quizzed Lee, but he only shrugged in response. Since she had avoided sending him back to Hel, he had lost the ability to just spirit up new clothing, so they had to make do. He felt guilty about it, but there was little in the way of options. 'Well, I just hope they can deliver,' Tessa muttered dubiously, the very idea of fetching a whole couch in her ancient car was a joke. It screeched and groaned simply holding people, let alone enormous pieces of furniture. "That or we have to strap it to the top of the Kingswood. I don't like our chances of getting it home if that's the case."

There were, of course, far greater concerns than her couch, but she tried not to think about it, especially when a lot of that stress centred around the delicious man standing before her.

Tessa wrapped her arms around Lee's neck and pulled him close, breathing in his unique scent before kissing him deeply. Lee returned the favour, placing both of his hands on her hips and pulling her closer still. Without her heels he easily stood a head taller than Tessa, something she absolutely loved. Her hands ran down his back before she brought one back up to cup the side of his face, running her fingers over his angular jaw and high cheekbones. This was the intimacy she craved whenever she was away from Lee, usually when she had to work.

Soon Lee's intense arousal became very apparent, an erection pulsing against the fabric of his pants. Tessa cheekily grinned and rubbed herself against it provocatively. She simply adored the growls that the simple act of seduction could draw from him and always wanted more. Shifting his hands to her butt, Lee easily lifted her so she could wrap her legs around him. Still lip locked Lee began to walk them both to the bedroom, unzipping the back of Tessa's dress as he went.

Lee was about to throw his prize down onto the bed when Tessa's phone rang with the registered Agency emergency only tone. She groaned loudly, sorely tempted to ignore the call, but she dutifully unhitched her legs and was gently placed back onto the floor. Holding the edges of her dress together, Tessa ran to grab her phone and hurriedly answered, trying not to sound disappointed.

'Lady Bale, a case has come in... for you... which requires immediate attention.' Sir McAdams' voice boomed down the line, making Tessa flinch and hold the phone a little further away. There must be something very wrong if her boss was shouting and wheezing this much.

'Ok Sir, I shall come in immediately. I will be twenty minutes.' Tessa responded dutifully, while sighing in annoyance.

'See that you do Lady Bale, this will be a very delicate case, requiring a... unique touch. I shall tell you more when you get to my office,' he finished and hung up immediately, avoiding all the usual pleasantries. Tessa sighed again and rubbed her forehead.

'Duty calls?' Lee asked, sneaking up behind her to zip up her dress again. He already knew the answer but asked anyway. Tessa nodded, reluctant to go. She knew she must, even if only to pay for a new couch.

'A new case apparently, something that has the man all hot under the collar,' Tessa replied, before grabbing her abandoned tea and pouring it down the sink.

'I'm all hot under the collar,' growled Lee, handing her the purse he had already retrieved from behind the TV. He anticipated that Tessa would never find it herself.

'But here's the thing hun, you will actually get your respite when I get back. I am pretty sure the Sir never gets any respite. Certainly not by the way he behaves,' she said sarcastically, before giving Lee a long kiss goodbye.

Chapter Two

It must have been a bad case Tessa thought, as Sir McAdams had only stopped to leer at Tessa twice while she was entering his office and sitting down. He was in his element as always, his pompous overweight mass wedged behind the huge wooden expanse of his table, which rumour has it, was mostly full of candy. He pushed the case file forward after greeting Tessa in his usual abrupt manner.

'Lady Bale, this case is one of extreme delicacy, hence why I have chosen you to cover it. It also bears some odd similarities to your previous case, so I believe you may bring some good insight also.' Tessa tried not to groan audibly, turning it into a strangled cough instead. The last thing she wanted was a case like the previous one, especially when the nightmares still woke her in the early hours of the morning.

'Yes Sir, what are they if you don't mind?' she asked, accepting the file. Upon opening the cover, she got her answer. Vacant dead eyes stared back at her, surrounded with carved flesh and anaemic skin. Tessa held her composure well, despite the brutal images now burning into her mind. Sir McAdams saw her reaction and grimaced himself, having seen the images already.

'Given that we can uhhh, safely exclude your previous case's suspect and no details were released from the case to the media, we can fairly safely say that this is someone killing on their own steam. The main issue is who the victim is,' he elaborated, giving Tessa time to look again and try to see who it was. It was largely impossible given the amount of trauma she had suffered. Tessa was still drawing a blank, so he continued. 'The victim is a rather well-known local witch celebrity, who runs a successful business from her skills and even does stints on

TV. Her name is Stacia Sing, and her business is SingSong Healing over in Upton. She has a rather extensive and affluent clientele base. It is for that reason we need this dealt with quietly and quickly. There is a... uhhh... link to this being a murder of magickal origin, and that is making everyone nervous. Use whatever you need, but get it done,' he commanded, looking sterner she had ever seen him before. Tessa swallowed hard, suddenly realising the gravity of the situation. *Why was she even chosen for this? Surely there were other more experienced hunters to be taking this one?*

'Yes Sir, I will Sir. Where is the body?' she guessed that was as good a start as any.

'You're in luck, we got onto this one fast, it's still at the scene, in situ. She was murdered sometime during the night; it was reported two hours ago by her shop hand who showed up for work and allegedly found her. The girl has been sent home, being too distraught to be of any use at the current time. You need to go there straight after you have been to see Lady Kirk for supplies. You are going to need them.' He nodded before turning back to his papers. That was that then. Tessa was dismissed. She didn't bother waiting for the cursory hand wave.

Lady Kirk's rooms were in their usual state of chaos, Sibyls rummaging through the latest deliveries and casting various magickal items everywhere. A few other Agents roamed around but the Lady herself was beaming at Tessa with her arms full of leaves, gently feeding them into a grinder.

'Tessa, darling, how is the healing?' she shouted over the whir of the grinder before throwing in the last of the rue. She switched the machine off with a flick of her boot and came over to greet Tessa properly.

'All done thanks to your amazing herbs Lady, they really did an excellent job. I almost didn't have an impressive scar to show off!' Tessa smiled at the closest thing she had to a friend. Hel, Lady Kirk was the only person at work to actually call her Tessa instead of Contessa or Lady Bale.

'Oh, because that's such a bad thing! Now what are you doing back here already? Shouldn't you still be off sick and mourning the loss of that hot demon?' giggled Lady Kirk, looking for all her age like a silly schoolgirl.

'Hah no, I have a case. Have barely thought about the demon actually. Been too busy sleeping and watching TV.' Tessa replied, nearly choking on the lie. Lying was hard for her at the best of times, even moreso when it came to Lady Kirk.

'You have been thrown a case already? But you've barely recovered from the last! Whoever authorised this? I will be giving them a piece of my mind.'

'I am well enough Lady, I promise. I really needed something else to do. Although I am not sure I really want this one.' Tessa fought futilely to quash the images which were popping up in her mind again. Lady Kirk raised an eyebrow and pursed her lips, clearly of two minds whether she wanted to ask about it. Tessa shook her head and saved her the shock.

'Now all I really need to stock up on is some cascarilla, ajenjible and some althea...' she trailed off, following Lady Kirk along the rows to collect her supplies before heading over to Upton and its newest little shop of horrors.

Chapter Three

The exterior of SingSong Healing was lovely, with plenty of purple paint, swirls of silver and crystals dangling everywhere. A small collection of tables and chairs sat out the front, they also had some kind of cafe arrangement going on. A jingling bell sounded as Tessa entered the store, breaking the buzz of noise produced by the mundane police officers waiting for her. Tessa nodded curtly, her tattoos identification enough for Law Enforcement. The two police men nodded back before the sacrificial lamb stepped forward.

'Bout time you Agency lot got here. Been waiting for you for hours with the damn stiff. I have things to do,' he snapped, his frown forcing his bushy eyebrows so low they almost covered his eyes completely.

'You mean Ms Sing, not the stiff, I am sure,' responded Tessa, already feeling incensed by his tone and crude manner.

'Yeah whatever. The dead witch. Fitting death for a freak like that,' he spat, crooking his finger at the other officer to follow him out. Tessa became furious, lashing out magick and dropping the temperature in the room until her breath condensed into mist.

'What was your name officer?' she requested, mentally slamming the door closed before they could leave. It hurt her head to use her magick so physically like this, but it needed to happen. A little fear of the hunters was almost advocated by the Agency, it helped to affirm their power as a law enforcement agency. Plus, Tessa was damn pissed off. The policeman merely snorted.

'That's sergeant.'

'Fine, SERGEANT, what is your name?' she demanded this time, sending out a tendril of magick to chill him more, resisting the urge to make it squeeze his throat until his head popped off.

'Sergeant Culpepper. What the hell is all this?' he yelped, as his extremities began to take on a blue tinge. Suddenly Tessa stopped, allowing the room to return to normal.

'All what Serg-eant?' she replied coquettishly, putting on an innocent drawl. He looked angrily to the other officer, who had felt nothing thanks to a nifty little shield Tessa had surrounded him with.

'It's damn witch tricks. God damned bunch of freaks, it's unnatural and ought to be stopped.' With that he turned on his heel and stalked out.

'I will be talking to your superior,' Tessa called after him, receiving an obscene gesture for her efforts as the other police officer shot her an apologetic look and scuttled out after him. She shrugged and locked the main door behind them, not really wanting to deal with any more attitude when she had a dead witch to investigate. Some people still resented those of magickal nature, with exactly the sergeant's reasoning.

According to the case file, the murder had occurred in the private residence behind the store, where Ms Sing lived. It was surprisingly modest, but she had apparently come from modest means. Tessa entered carefully, taking note of all around her and pulling out her camera. She snapped away at the disturbed table and chairs, clearly knocked aside in a struggle, as well as blood drips and smears on the floor and walls.

A few pieces of mail in Ms Sing's name had been strewn across the floor, so Tessa carefully took a picture of that too. It seemed that Stacia had put up quite the fight, and Tessa hoped that she had wounded whoever had attacked her. Mundane forensics would test all the blood residue for them to determine if that had been the case.

Finally, Tessa found her, a frail little body left lying in the kitchen. Her various jars of herbs had all been smashed, and Tessa took the time to take pictures of all the debris before finally turning to the body. Ms Sing had clearly been turned this way and that as cuts in her flesh were made to carve various sigils and patterns. Her tiny body was coated in the same blood that was congealed in puddles on the floor, and those strange grey eyes just staring blindly forth.

Tessa sent out feelers for magick, but it was all surprisingly sterile. There was simply nothing there, aside from the gentle protective magick on the house itself. She supposed that whatever nasty act the carvings were intended for wore off fast, so took a closer look to see if there were any clues in the cuttings themselves. The more she looked the more confused she became at their nonsense.

Here was an eye, there a letter and some zigzags, but none of it seemed to mean anything to her. She dug out her phone to call her brain trust, on his brand-new phone. She could only hope he had finally turned on. It rang on and on before Lee finally answered, just as she was about to hang up.

'Hello Hel cat, need me already huh?'

'NO! But yeah. This is another case with a real artistic butcher, but I can't make sense of what they have cut. I need you to tell me if you know of anything in your experience. Should I send over some pictures?' she asked, praying that he would have an easy answer.

'Are you there now?'

'Yes? Why?'

'Oh, never mind about the pictures, I can do one better.' His voice full of cheeky mystery.

'Huh?' Tessa asked quizzically, but it was too late, he had hung up. Suddenly the air next to her shifted and Lee stepped out, narrowly missing the largest blood patch.

'Woah... what the Hel?' she asked, feeling just a little unsettled. Lee just shrugged.

'Eh well the planes of existence have different lengths. I just use one that is faster to get to where you are. Blood beacon and all that.'

He scratched his horns idly as he always did when he thought. Tessa nodded before shrugging it off too and getting back to the task at hand. The physics was beyond her comprehension when a dead body lay so close.

'So, I can see an eye, this looks like a pyramid, and another, perhaps this is a rune... tyr maybe? But none of it adds up to me. What do you think?' she asked, gazing up at him. Moments passed as he stepped this way and that, looming over the remains of Ms Sing with grave focus.

'Well, I can tell you now, it's utter shit,' he concluded firmly. Tessa's jaw dropped.

'So, it really isn't anything?' she queried, not quite ready to believe it was as simple as that.

'Nope. Looks like a three-year-old was let loose with a crayon. It's all just shapes and a poor mockery of magickal work. Looks like you have a fake dear,' he said flatly, clearly unimpressed by their efforts.

Tessa stewed on the implications of this discovery as she took the pictures to prove it. Upon closer inspection of the cuts to the chest she realised they were covering up three deep stab wounds, any of which could have killed Stacia Sing. She then donned gloves and searched around and under the body, but yielded nothing. No magickal accoutrements or bags, just a body and a lot of congealed blood.

Tessa and Lee then worked together to search the rest of the house, but there was nothing of interest to be found. It appeared whoever had done this had left the rest of the house undisturbed. Every sweet little potted plant, frilled cushion and even stuffed toys were neatly placed and blood free. This cosy witchy utopia had been marred forever. Even the magick whispered of pain, slowly diminishing with the loss of the witch who cast it.

Finally, Tessa called in the magickal forensic and cleanup crew to finish the job. As she was packing up her last few investigative tools, a cat came running in and began to twine wildly around Lee's legs. He almost squealed in excitement as he picked it up, straight away cradling it like a baby and tickling its stomach while cooing. Tessa rolled her eyes at the behaviour, awed at the big intimidating demon turning into a cooing mess over a black cat.

'We will have to see if Stacia has any family to take it,' she explained while walking up to give it a scratch under the chin. Immediately it began a roar of a purr, looking up at Tessa with oddly mismatched eyes. 'Woah... does that cat have one blue eye and one green eye? Freaky!' she exclaimed while scratching it behind the ears much to its delight.

'Don't you know, cats and demons have been friends for eternity. It's said it is because they can see through the planes, while we walk them. Can we keep it?' he asked, looking at her earnestly.

'Noooo, we cannot steal a murder victim's cat! She may have family for it to go to; I will have to contact them. The cat goes to them!' she chastised as Lee became more and more endearing in his behaviour.

'But what if she gets left here all alone?' Two sets of eyes were now pleading to Tessa, both the mismatched and the demonic. It was an onslaught not even she could fight. 'Ok we will take her for now, but when we find them, it goes to the family,' she affirmed as a bell rang out from the front door of the shop.

'That's probably clean-up. You better go... back the way you came?' she questioned, Lee grinning like mad over the cat still. He nodded dutifully and winked out of existence, cat included. How it remained calm while literally walking through different planes of reality was beyond her, but it was a witch's cat after all. There was probably very little that surprised it any more, after all it seemed to be smart enough to hide somewhere in this little cottage until it was safe.

On the way out of the home cottage, Tessa noted a small walkway beside the shop, so one could access the house without going through the business. She made a note to investigate it after she let the crew in. The store itself seemed as it should be, nothing knocked over or defaced, all the money and an appointment book present. Clearly neither money nor Ms Sing's contacts had been the target. Even all the stock was undisturbed.

This had clearly been all about Stacia Sing, nothing else. That blew the theory of this being a murder to get to her rich and famous contacts out of the water. Tessa idly wondered if her mother Irina was in the book but was reticent to find out. At this point she did not want to know anything that her family was up to, as long as it didn't involve her... or any more attempts on her life.

Passing back through the shop, Tessa let the clean-up crew in, part forensics crew, part post murder cleaners. In magickal murders it was sometimes safer to keep the cleaning in house. Rogue spells caused havoc for the mundane crime scene cleaners, and most things magickal spooked them.

After handing over the scene and pointing out areas she wanted them to focus on, Tessa took the booking diary from the store. She seriously hoped that some little clue lay within its pages, because there was very little to go on currently. If she saw note of her mother, she could just pass the task onto Sir McAdams. She gave one last cursory look over the cottage and left.

The alley beside the shop revealed nothing, being floored in cobblestone and resistant to footprints. A quick scan left nothing much to find from her perspective, a fancy wrought iron gate blocked it off very effectively. She notified the forensics crew about the alley, and they promised they would contact her if they found anything of interest in the alley or the house.

Chapter Four

Tessa's next port of call was to visit the shop hand, whose address had been left with the police. Missy Pierce had worked with Stacia since this store had opened, about five years ago. She had also worked at a previous store Stacia had managed, before going out on her own and opening SingSong Healing. That was the sum total of the information that the mundane police had bothered to record. Still, Tessa was surprised they had managed that much given their attitude.

Missy answered the door with her dark gothic makeup smudged all over her face and a mauled tissue twisting in her hands. Her hands shook as she greeted Tessa, before showing her into the living room. Tessa noted quietly that every light in the house was on, a clear sign this poor girl was scared senseless. People were funny how they sought their various comforts.

Before she had even begun her questioning Tessa had ruled the girl out as the killer. She quivered in her seat and tortured the tissue further in her hands as Tessa began to interview her. Even her piercings were red and swollen from being wiped or picked at. White face powder was smudged onto the corseted black dress she wore, smudged on the flared sleeves from wiping away tears. She even still clutched her keys, the black spiderwebbed lanyard hanging from her pale hands.

'So, you worked at a previous venue together before Stacia opened her store and poached you too, is there any way that store's owner is holding a grudge?'

'Not at all. They closed the store, which is why we left. They loved Stacia and even helped her navigate the opening of her own store.' The answer came thick with sniffles, but Tessa was patient.

'What about rivals? Business or personal?'

'No, the only store like us just posts sort of ranty things on their website. We mostly ignore them, and I doubt they would ever do something like this. The way she was... c-c-cut... No one would do that. It really happened though, didn't it?' The poor girl sought validation from Tessa, trying to affirm that it had been as horrific as she had witnessed. Her grey-green eyes were overwhelmed with tears again.

'It was very real I am afraid. But I am here to find out what happened to her and take down the one who did it. Can you take me through what happened today?' Tessa spoke with grim determination.

'It was the same as any day. Well, I thought so, but Stacia is usually way ahead of me in opening up. It was all dark, so I went in, turned everything on and set up. When she didn't come in after an hour, I knew there was... something... wrong.' Missy took a moment to sob hysterically again while Tessa made soothing noises. She eventually calmed down and continued with a voice now torn ragged. 'I went out the back, to the cottage. I have a spare key just in case. I called for her, over and over. She, she didn't answer, so I went in and saw all that blood. I fell down, then I just freaked out. Somehow, I must have called someone to help, because then there were police there. I don't remember anything after that. I guess I got home somehow. I have just kinda sat here since.' Missy sort of waved an arm around to emphasise her black armchair, covered in black doilies. The keys jingled in her hand as it went.

'So, you were here all night before that?' Tessa asked more for formality than suspicion.

'Last night I went out with my girlfriend. We went to a restaurant. Ummm something Nepalese. She stayed the night until I had to leave for work. We do it once a week. A date night kinda thing.' Missy over explained in her nervousness. Convinced her alibi would check out, Tessa noted down the number of the girlfriend directly off Missy's phone, saved with a little love heart beside it. It was all she could do to bring the number up with shaky fingers and pass across the phone. The woman was a wreck.

There was unfortunately very little else to say, and nothing that would soothe Missy. Tessa left with promises to communicate should anything come up. As she walked out of the semi-squalid apartment block, she called the girlfriend's number.

'Hello?' The voice was timid, wary.

'Hello, my name is Tessa Bale, I work for the Agency and I am investigating an incident with Missy Pierce. When did you see her last?' There was a gasp on the other end of the line.

'Missy, is she ok? I only left a few hours ago. Is she hurt? What happened? Where is she?' Gone was all timidity, this was now a gale force peppering of questions.

'She is fine, I just needed to know where she was last night and this morning.'

'So, she is a suspect? She was with me all that time. I promise, she ain't do it.' The girlfriend fell into a more slum accent as she became stressed and defensive.

'No, I am just checking for her. What was your name please?'

'Susan Betty. So, she is ok?'

'Yes Susan, she is just very upset. You may need to go to her, if you have that kind of relationship. She found Stacia this morning.' Tessa explained carefully.

'Found her? She works for her? What do you mean?'

Of course she didn't know. Tessa cringed reflexively, realising her mistake.

'Stacia passed away this morning. I am the Agency officer who is investigating her death. Is there anything you can tell me about the relationship between Stacia and Missy?' Tessa figured that she might as well start investigating while she had a captive listener.

'Nuffin.'

'I don't believe she did it,' Tessa said with a smile.

'Ok, Stacia was like a mother. She supported us, and always had us for dinner. She was gonna be the one to marry us, I was plannin' it with her. Was a secret for Missy. I hid a ring there. Oh no, the ring! It has a cat on it! Is it there?" Tessa was tempted to giggle at the image, but stifled it as she unlocked her car and threw her bag in.

"It doesn't look like anything was stolen, if you can give me an idea of where it was hidden, I can go check in the next few days."

"Please, she done hid it behind a pot plant. The Hamamelis. It's a mini one, got yellow kinda flowers now that look all raggedy. It's a shiny black pot." Susan was earnest and sincere, Tessa instantly liked her. She resolved to get the ring when she could, it was the least she could do for these sweet kids. Even after she said her goodbyes, Tessa took a moment to sit in her car. It had been an emotionally overwhelming case already, and it was just the first day. Somehow, she had to stop getting shunted the particularly bloody cases.

With little else to do for now, she headed back home to begin reviewing the day's work.

Lee and the odd eyed cat were curled up in the bed together when Tessa got home, and a vast collection of brand-new feline paraphernalia sat in the corner. She rubbed her head tiredly, sensing the cat was now here to stay and wondering how she would explain that one to the family. She also regretted letting Lee loose with her debit card.

A quick check of her emails revealed nothing had turned up in the preliminary forensics, and Sir McAdams seconded Lee's theory that the sigils and carvings seemed to be senseless. His recommendation that Tessa summon a demon for help on the case was quickly skipped over guiltily. She cued up the photos she had taken today to print so she could begin to study them and headed into the kitchen to hunt for food.

Finally, Lee woke and appeared as the kettle boiled, giving Tessa a kiss as he rifled through the fridge himself. Meanwhile the cat had padded in and began to wash itself, and Tessa laughed at how ridiculously domestic and odd the scene appeared. As if realising her sudden contentment in normalcy, her phone beeped with an urgent text message from the Agency.

CHECK UPTON NEWS IMMEDIATELY. SIR MCADAMS

Feeling confused and apprehensive Tessa loaded the website for the Upton News Network. A glaring headline caught her attention, not that she could have missed it:

Magickal Murder Targets Famous Helper of 'Mundanes'

Tessa read on, the article citing a police source as having revealed that Stacia Sing had been murdered in a magickal ritual, and she had long been a helper of non magickal folk to both understand magick and utilise it in small ways. The article stated repeatedly that there was a magickal murderer, and already the comments were racking up. After the fifth threat against magickal folk as a whole, Tessa decided to step away from the Internet for her own sanity. She called Sir McAdams to reassure him that no, it was not an Agency leak, and yes, she probably knew exactly who it was. Sergeant Culpepper would get a nice little suspension notice in the morning. That at least cheered Tessa up, not that it was likely to change his attitude. Some bigots never change, and the hate always managed to spread.

Tessa allowed herself to settle in for a nice night of curling up with Lee and the cat while reviewing the gristly murder scene photos. Lee took it upon himself to massage both her and the cat, and Tessa again allowed herself to dream of the lovely domesticity this moment gave. They may be able to make it yet, just a normal couple living a life together. Well, as normal as a demon and a witch could be.

Chapter Five

By the next morning forensics had revealed that while Stacia Sing had put up a good fight, she had not apparently managed to maim her killer. It was only her own blood spread all over the small cottage. She also did not appear to have any family on either the Agency's or the mundane record systems. Her parents appear to have died when she was young, and she had apparently never married or even lived with anyone else. Her will benefited only Missy Pierce, who would take over ownership of the shop in the event of her death and continue its good work. She also had to keep the cat, but it had apparently 'run away' overnight.

Missy hadn't even known she would get the store, let alone the entire estate, so had certainly not murdered Stacia Sing for it. Tessa was back at square one; brutal murder, fake magick and no suspects.

After breakfast Tessa and Lee reread everything they had on the case, but nothing stood out. Frustrated and stuck at a dead end, Tessa paced the room, thinking as she went. Their training hadn't really covered what to do in the absence of magick. Eventually she gave up, grabbing her bag and Lee in order to go couch shopping.

His horns safely stowed in a baggy beanie, Lee managed to merely look like a rather tall and gorgeous human. Initially Tessa had been afraid to let him out but eventually conceded on the proviso that he hid his horns. They were, after all; the defining feature of demonhood. They had finally settled on a couch after much debate and Tessa was just paying up when she heard a familiar slimy voice molest her ears.

'Well Con-tessa, your new case is already in the news and you're out shopping. That sounds about right. Already too much for you?'

Mike Schimpf sidled up to her, Tessa turning to face him while Lee tried to disappear as best he could, pulling his beanie down further and pretending to be just another customer in the queue.

'What are you doing here Slimy Schimpf-ey?' asked Tessa, thoroughly over his attitude, but trying to keep his attention on her, rather than those around her.

'Always back chatting like a rude little teenager, aren't you? I have actually earned some time off if you must know. Spending my bonus for another stellar case,' he said, puffing out his chest over his scrawny belly. It was a day off and he still wore an ugly brown wool suit and a stained button up shirt. Everything fitted poorly, testament to his massive recent weight loss. Tessa snorted loudly.

'Whatever, I have better things to do than listen to you verbally masturbate. Toddle on Schimpf-ey. Playtime's over,' with that she turned back to the teller to organise delivery. Mike Schimpf stood floundered a few seconds, looking at everyone around him including Lee, who ducked his face down, before stalking away. Tessa finally released the breath she had been holding and together they beat a hasty retreat.

Tessa and Lee bolted home as fast as the old Kingswood would allow, only feeling at ease when behind closed doors. They silently went about their business, Tessa preparing to go back to the shop to interview Missy again and Lee busying himself around the apartment. Missy had text messaged earlier to say that she had remembered something else, and could Tessa come around to hear it. The girl seemed too afraid to leave the shop alone. Tessa had no choice but to leave Lee to his brooding and travelled across town again.

SingSong Healing was as beautiful as she had remembered it, but now its beauty was marred by the collection of newspaper and TV reporters and cameras out the front. Cursing, Tessa pushed through the crowd, pondering whether Missy had set her up with the press. She threw that idea out immediately when she saw the girl in question.

Pale and haunted, Missy hadn't bothered with makeup, revealing dark circles under her eyes and sallow skin. She wrung her hands constantly while she greeted Tessa and got her a tea.

'I had to message you when I remembered other things about what happened when... when I found her. Did you know she had no children? I have no parents, well I was given up for adoption, grew up in the system. Then I scored this job, and Stacia... she became like a mother to me. Apparently, she left me all this, but, I don't think I can ever go into the cottage again. I just see her every time, her eyes. That smell.' Missy began to cry in earnest again. Tessa handed her a tissue from her purse, jumping on the mention of a smell but trying to keep her patience. There hadn't really been one when Tessa had done her initial investigation, aside from the many drying herbs in the cottage.

'Smell? Was there something out of the ordinary?' Tessa probed gently, giving her the time to compose herself.

'It smelled fruity... but it was sickly sweet then underneath that, it was like the most wretched body odour. It was awful,' Missy said balefully. Tessa nodded gently, noting it down in her little notebook. The stench of the unwashed and something sickly sweet... hopefully this was the scent of the murderer, although it had to be strong to have lasted since the murder occurred. Either that or the murderer had just left when Missy thought to check on Stacia. It may be luck that she was still alive.

"Did you hear anything at all? Someone leaving?"

"No, its pretty quiet there, that's why Stacia chose to build the cottage." Missy felt calm enough to sip her tea gently, and Tessa was reminded about her promise to look for the ring. She excused herself quickly to have another look at the cottage and the access alley. Now the body was gone the small abode was much more welcoming and pleasant, much like Stacia Sing would have kept it in life. The cleanup crew had done an excellent job, no hint of the body or the blood remained. Tessa went over the place for any last clues, including poking through her personal items just in case, but she had no luck finding anything out of the ordinary. She did manage to find the witchhazel plant, with its raggedy yellow flowers. It was squeezed into a corner in Stacia's bedroom, and there was still a little box hidden in the gap behind it. Tessa couldn't help but open it to take a cheeky look. Inside was a gorgeous ring, the band a leaping cat with a heart shaped ruby in the centre. She pocketed it, knowing that the Agency system would take forever to release the ring as it was technically part of the crime scene.

Tessa tried the alley next, pulling out her little torch to really get a good look. Considering this was the most likely candidate for an entry and exit to the little alcove where the cottage lay, she wanted to take extra care. Forensics had already had a look, but Tessa always liked to check again, they tended to only look in the common areas. She found many stray blood spots, probably flicked by a boot or clothing on the run out. Finally, she hit pay dirt. On the underside of one of the delicately wrought leaves of the iron gate was a tiny blood smudge with a short blonde hair stuck in it. Neither Stacia Sing nor Missy Pierce were blonde, and it was on the inside of the gate that few had access to. It was hopefully a good nab on the killer, and Tessa carefully bagged it and labelled it after taking a picture.

Elated that she had *something* to go on, Tessa finished up her search and turned to leave. It was only then that she realised she was not alone in the alley, and without the key to the gate she had no escape.

Chapter Five

The demon was tall, a good 9 inches over 6 foot and well-armed. His face was scarred heavily, adding to his intimidating appearance that the angry scowl perfected.

'Where is he?' the demon snarled as he walked up to stand over her, obsidian horns glinting in the dappled sunlight that entered the alley. Unusually, his horns had been polished and pointed wickedly, curling back around his head and making his whole demanour even scarier. Everything about this demon was intimidating, right down to the all-black clothing.

'Wh-where is who?' Tessa tried to plead innocent, her heart sinking. She knew exactly who he meant.

'Don't even try little witch. You stink of him. Where is Lee Stanrael?' replied the demon, backing her into the gate and standing directly over her. She was close enough to see the scars on his chest that poked out of his leather vest and smell the faint scent of sulphur and man.

'He went back. I did the ritual.'

'No, he didn't. You stuffed up little witch. I will find him. When I do, he is coming back, dead or alive.' With that the demon turned and winked out of existence, walking between planes. Tessa exhaled sharply before bolting out of the alley and home as fast as she could manage.

She burst into the door to find Lee making something in the kitchen.

'There is some crazy scarred up demon after you. He called you Lee Stanrael. He is going to kill you!' Tessa gibbered to him from the doorway, still so terrified by her encounter. He ran to her and drew her into his arms, embracing her tightly.

'I was afraid of this. They have released him. He is a very old demon, a hunter of rogues and enforcer of Hel. I don't know what his real name is, or if he ever had one, but he is known as Berserk. Did he have pointed horns?' Tessa could only nod in response, sniffling slightly.

'That's definitely him. He carved them up himself to keep them like that. We won't have long before he comes to take me.' Lee continued quietly. Tessa began to silently cry, grateful for the fact her face was buried in his chest.

'I have truly loved my time here, and you have changed my existence. After an eternity alive, I have finally lived. You made it so.' He put a finger under her chin and lifted her face before kissing her on the lips. He wordlessly thanked Tessa for all she had given him, and she kissed back, receiving the gratitude. She grabbed the back of his head, deepening the kiss and pressed her body against his. He took the hint, picking her up again to take her to the bedroom, pausing at the door for a few seconds just to make sure no one would call this time.

Lee carefully laid her on the bed before slowly pulling off her shoes and her stockings, kissing his way up from her toes. When he reached her skirt, he pulled it off gently, to continue kissing up her thighs. He watched as she spread her legs slightly to invite him further. Instead, he began to tease, kissing up to her underwear, taking it off carefully and kept kissing up the smooth expanse of her belly. Tessa's blouse was slowly unbuttoned as Lee trailed kisses up her stomach, which he knew threatened to drive her mad. She writhed on the bed, begging him to stop his teasing, but it fell on deaf ears.

He pulled off her blouse and undid her bra, sliding it slowly down her long arms, kissing every inch he met.

Lee returned to lay kisses directly over where her heart lay, before cradling and gently kissing each breast and nipple. When his tongue began to flick over them Tessa moaned loudly, much to her own surprise. She had never known a lover like this. Certainly not one who could make her moan before he had even gotten anywhere near her more erogenous zones.

He ran a series of kisses up the side of her neck, the sensation of his soft lips sending shivers down her spine.

Lee began to intersperse the kisses with erotic little nips, little flares of pain which only served to make Tessa wetter. Finally, he met her lips, and in the same movement gently but firmly thrust his entire length in, almost making her scream in the ecstasy of finally receiving what she had begged for. He stretched her, almost to the limit of what she could take, but at the same time it felt like she was complete. Tessa was lost in the sensation, her back arched up to feel every part.

Taking a firm hold of her hips he began to move, long smooth strokes into her as she fell back onto the bed. Looking up at him, Tessa marvelled at his incredible body, strong without being overly muscular and just enormous.

As he gazed down at her, Lee admired her red hair, splayed across the pillows and the slight sheen of sweat that was making her body glow. He thrust faster, their bodies moving in unison as Tessa began to feel a familiar heat and tingle rise from her feet. Kneeling now, Lee pulled Tessa completely off the bed as he pounded into her, close to orgasm himself. The heat in Tessa rose until it was overwhelming, before the dam broke and she came wildly, toes pointed and uncontrollably crying out.

The sight and glory of her pleasure had Lee coming just seconds later, slick on the results of her orgasm, thrusting hard and long until every last drop had been pumped into Tessa. He gently fell on top of her, taking care not to crush her as he gave a last few twitches inside her before laying still. For a few moments they simply panted together, both trying to catch their breath while completely entwined. He wiped some stray sweat off his brow before kissing her again. This time it was soft and caring, a promise of what neither were game to say.

Tessa sighed happily, content to just lie with him still inside her, wrapped in each other's arms. Long moments passed like that, with neither party willing to break the contact.

'Hel cat, you never cease to amaze,' said Lee, with his usual wicked grin spreading across his face. Tessa simply nodded, feeling utterly elated and replete. Worrying about Berserk would have to wait. For now, there was only bliss, which they explored fully.

Chapter Six

When Tessa headed into the Agency a little later, she still worried that they still hadn't discussed what to do about Berserk. After dropping her prized hair into forensics, she headed over to the archives. She was searching for any information on demons that they hadn't been taught in the classes she had taken. There was very little in the commonly used texts, given that the demons they commonly used were rather compliant and were mostly sent back voluntarily.

Those who went rogue were dealt with by a special team of elite hunters, for an elite prey. Exhausting the supply of newer publications, Tessa resorted to searching through the older tomes of the restricted section. Eventually she discovered a thick volume on Demonology that had been pushed to the back of the shelf, complete with a heavy coating of dust and a spider web. As she pulled it down, a plume of white dust fell over her, covering her in powder and making her sneeze repeatedly. Cussing wildly about lax librarian Sibyls, Tessa carried the book over to her little table and began to scan through to find a vanquishing or banishing spell.

As she flicked through the book, a page caught her eye, an entire plate image dedicated to Berserk. He was apparently a famous enough demon to warrant individual publication, which was highly unusual. Just as she was about to read the chapter, her phone rang loudly with the Agency emergency tone, much to the ire of the residing library Sibyl. Tessa scowled back as she answered, the dust still tickling her nose. She began praying that it was just a result on her hair but knew better than that.

'Lady Bale, you have another one. It seems like the killer has moved onto mundanes. Get there and get this done NOW. Address to follow.' With that Sir McAdams hung up, clearly not interested in discussing it. Tessa felt her heart sink with every word, knowing another person was dead on her watch. A mundane one at that.

Seconds later her phone beeped, directing her to a place on the border of North Bayton and Upton, in a developing area. Sneaking a furtive glance at the library sibyl, Tessa stuffed the Demonology book into her bag while she wasn't looking and quickly left.

On the way over to the address of her latest nightmare Tessa called Lee, letting him know where she was headed and why. In the back of her mind she knew she was checking up on him more than anything. The thought flittered through her worryingly, *what if Berserk found out where she lived and attacked him while she was out?* She felt completely powerless, even if logic told her that she was no match for an insanely strong and actually immortal demon executioner.

Still, she just had to trust that Lee would manage, and there was another murder to deal with on her end. As she drove through the neighbourhood Tessa was confronted by the cleanliness and safety such a suburb usually afforded. The houses were neat, there were little corner coffee shops and parks scattered around. Children played in the various open spaces and parents walked around in beige tones. It was a world away from her own neighbourhood. Even the street that the murder house lay on was exemplar, with neat gardens that even had frivolous things such as statues.

The outside of the house seemed nondescript enough, in that way that mild mannered, upwardly mobile suburbia is. Tessa shivered slightly, both for her hatred of the lifestyle of the average suburbanite and the impending murder scene. As with last time there were mundane police officers in attendance, mostly milling around while waiting for an Agent. Fearing a response like the last time, Tessa squared her shoulders and straightened her back before walking over with mock bravado. One officer stepped forward to greet her, a welcoming smile peeking out of his grim face.

'Hello ma'am, good of you to come.' Tessa scanned his face and words for sarcasm, confused at his nice demeanour. Finding none, she took his offered hand and gave it a firm shake.

'No problem, my name is Tessa. What do I have to look forward to?' she asked, trying to steel herself for the inevitable.

'I am Inspector Morris and it's sure not pretty. She is all hacked up, and they uh, used her blood on the walls. Some magickal script. Kept my people out in case it's some kind of booby trap or something. We kinda waited for you to get here just in case,' he explained, running his shaking hands over his buzz cut. That was why they were all spooked and loitering in the front garden. The neighbours were having a field day, judging by all the twitching curtains.

Tessa nodded, just because the last scene was a magickal hoax didn't mean this one was. Smart officer. Perhaps there was some better training happening nowadays. He certainly looked young for an Inspector, having barely grown out his baby fluff.

'Thanks. Is she a witch?' Tessa asked, thinking back to poor Stacia Sing, desperate for a connection.

'Nope she is a human. Name's Angelica Farr. Lives alone, only family is an elderly father. The only connection we have is a business card from SingSong Healing, which is why we had to call the Agency,' came the reply, making Tessa flinch. Witches were still human, a concept many mundanes didn't quite catch on to. Still, this was better than the overt hate that was normally thrown. She thanked the inspector kindly and nodded to the other milling officers as they began to disperse. This was now an Agency matter, and she had complete control over the scene.

As she turned her attention to the front door of the house, she realised it was slightly ajar. The stench of blood was there along with sickly sweet undertones, but she couldn't feel any magick yet. Inside the door lay a long hall, with doors branching off on either side. She checked them each one by one, but they all seemed undisturbed. She finally entered what appeared to be a beautiful sunroom, however the light was dappled red. The glass walls and even the roof was painted with blood lettering. Before she entered the room fully, Tessa sent out sneaky feelers of her own magick to sense any other.

Nothing, the room was dead.

Well, in more ways than one.

No booby traps, no ritual residue, nothing at all.

She walked in confidently and scanned the room as she took out her camera. Snapping away, Tessa scanned the area, taking in every pattern of blood flow and spray, every line of 'artwork' made. The remains of Ms Farr were crumpled in the corner, as if they were almost secondary to the greater tableau of the fake magick. In a way it really was, Tessa got the feeling the murderer wanted the occult nature to be more of a focus than the actual murder. She carefully picked her way over to the body, hopping over the evidence and capturing it on her camera as she did.

Ms Angelica Farr had clearly been a rather plain woman, unlike the somewhat glamorous Stacia Sing. Mousy brown hair was matted with blood and a pair of bent metal framed glasses lay nearby. Pale and freckled skin was torn up by a series of slashes, similar to the last murder but certainly not the same. Here and there they had attempted letters again, but it mostly seemed to be randomised lines. By the angle of the cuts and the feathering at the ends the person who had made the cuts was clearly right-handed, not that the information really helped.

There were slight hand marks printed in blood on her body, however lack of prints and presence of fold lines pointed to gloves. Tessa couldn't really blame them for wanting to use gloves, there was certainly a lot of blood around. The poor girl had practically been bled dry.

Tucked into her hand, devoid of blood, was the card to SingSong Healing. It had clearly been placed there on purpose. It was simply a message, to force the narrative the killer was trying to create. Whether she liked it or not, that card was now evidence.

Tessa took the necessary pictures of the body and then carefully rolled it over to see if there was anything underneath, crouching beside it to get a close look. Suddenly the body gave a sad and beleaguered sigh, making Tessa jump back in shock and pull her knife.

Chapter Seven

T essa stood and stared at the body for long moments, knife drawn and every muscle tense. Her heart hammered erratically in her chest. She waited, expecting the corpse to start to get up or make another sound. The memories of her previous case certainly didn't help her paranoid thoughts.

When nothing more happened, she relaxed, allowing rational thoughts to settle in her scattered mind. Of course, moving the body had caused an air expulsion from the lungs, coming out as a large sigh. Tessa shook her head and put her knife away, feeling a little silly at her freak out.

With her hands still shaking, she knelt back down, her eyes scanning across the underside of the body and the floor beneath it. There was nothing that jumped out to her, and she was starting to run out of ideas.

Inspector Morris called from the hallway to see if it was safe to enter, poking his head around the doorway when given the "all clear".

'Your Agency forensics lot are here now so my crew are going to take off, a few human murders need looking at. Anything else you need just give me a call, I will send over a report from our end too. Er, good luck with it,' Morris empathised, looking dubiously around the room. Tessa nodded and bid him farewell as the forensics crew trooped in, carefully picking their way around the evidence in their little booties. Tessa informed them about moving the body and showed them the pictures she took before stepping back and watching them work.

While waiting for a preliminary response, she called the Agency and was patched through to the forensic offices to enquire about her precious golden hair. They had looked at it and confirmed that the murderer was indeed a natural blonde, as well as they were probably male, but that was all they could offer as the hair had no root. So DNA was a bust, at least for now. Tessa sighed and drummed her fingers on her lower lip, feeling frustrated.

The three members of the forensic crew had split up, one going over the body, one inspecting the art on the walls and another doing a more general check.

Tessa loved to watch them work, their methods containing not only traditional methods such as dusting and DNA, but also magickal testing. There was a spray that could make magickal auras and trails visible as well as gizmos to detect the unique signature of the magick used and power level. Suddenly her phone rang again, shrilling through the silence and making everyone jump. Tessa apologised profusely and smiled when she realised it was Lee calling. She bolted out of earshot before answering.

'Hey Hel cat, how is it looking over there?' asked Lee, his voice clearly distracted and hedging around something.

'Disgusting actually. I mean most murder scenes are, but this is exceptional. This time they drew on the wall in blood. All this nonsensical stuff, crazy lines and squiggles. There is nothing magickal there at all, I am sure of it,' Tessa responded, placing her hand on her hip for emphasis before she remembered that he couldn't actually see her.

'Aye, and I am sure you're right.'

'I know I am... I think,' Tessa said, not willing to completely commit to her conviction.

'Yeah and uh, how are you?' His question made Tessa curious as to what he was up to.

'I'm just fine, why do you ask?' she said suspiciously.

'Oh nothing, just thought I would make sure you're ok and all. Haven't had any problems today or anything,' came the rather flippant reply. Now she knew something was up, and she knew exactly what it was.

'Well, I ripped a nail off, had to file it and I even got a stone caught in my shoe, but no, there have not been any obsidian horned problems in my day.' Tessa felt sassy, but still checked over her shoulder as if her words could call him into existence.

'Ah uh... yeah. Well I hope it stays that way. I have been thinking about it a lot. I just can't think of how we can beat him. Or send him back. Someone has sent him over here who knows I didn't return. How can we beat this?' Lee was getting higher and higher pitched as he bordered on tears, suddenly making Tessa wish she could be with him. She had no idea he was this worried, or that they were really in that much danger. The sheer concept of Lee crying was foreign to her. For this demon to be scared, it had to be serious.

'We will deal with it, I promise. I have an old book from the Agency archives on Demonology, so I am sure we can find something in that.'

'Lady Bale!' A voice from the house called, making Tessa jump guiltily. She turned around to see one of the forensics people leaning out of the back door. Her little blonde head peeked out of the door, but for the life of her, Tessa could not remember her name.

'Y-yes?' she responded guiltily, leaving Lee to wait on the line.

'We done found no trace of magick, so we gonna proceed with them mundane level ok?" The forensics tech was simply asking permission to go onto the next step of investigation. Tessa released the breath she had been holding in before answering, still a little shaky.

'Yes, that's what I expected, thank you.' The girl disappeared back indoors, leaving Tessa to quickly wrap up her conversation with Lee and head in after her. She had been unnerved by almost being caught and wanted to ask them something while she remembered it.

'Hey guys?' she addressed the room in general, waiting until all three faces had turned to her before continuing. 'Did any of you smell anything when you came in, or even now for that matter?' Tessa had almost forgotten about Missy and her smells, but Lee had reminded her before he hung up. The two men shook their heads, but the woman tentatively put up her hand. Tessa nodded and pointed to her, feeling a bit like a schoolteacher.

'Yes, Lady, I done smelt... I did smell something, was really sweet but not nice, and kind of stinky.' Tessa smiled at her use of the Bayton slum lingo, clearly this was another Agency success story.

'Ok that's excellent. Can you think of anything it smells like?'

'Yeah, smelled like me mum, she stink'n like that cause she got diabetes the Doc says.' As the young girl spoke, Tessa's mind ticked over rapidly. That would make a lot of sense, when diabetics didn't monitor the disease well, they often began to smell odd as their bodies excreted the sugars that built up in their blood. Some people described it as acetone, some as rotten fruit with added chenicals. Tessa could have slapped herself it was so obvious. She thanked the girl and took her leave, with the promise of the reports to follow.

Thus far they were looking at a male diabetic with blonde hair and a pathetic idea of what magick really was. At least now she could start hitting up medical records, especially as there was only one hospital in Bayton, and most diabetics were treated there. Few could afford the fees to attend the private hospital in Upton, or travel to Birmingdale where the next public hospital was.

On her was home she got patched through to the hospital, then transferred to medical records. She requested copies of all files of male diabetics to be sent to the Agency, immediately feeling sorry for the poor bastard who had to fulfil that request. They reassured her it would be done overnight, a doozy for the night staff, and she would have them on the morrow. Tessa thanked them curtly, cutting the call as she was pulling up to her apartment block. Just as she stepped out of her car she noticed a familiar silhouette walking down the street, away from her. She called after him, knowing how good a help he may be.

'Damien, dammit DAMIEN!' She began to run to catch up, hindered by her heels. He sped up into a sprint and disappeared down an alley, which was empty by the time she got there, puffing and panting. Angrily she kicked some loose concrete shouting down the empty length.

'You gutless worm, people are dying damn you! Get over your pride.' No answer came, forcing Tessa to give up and retreat home sulkily.

Lee's eyes nearly popped out of his head when Tessa pulled the tattered Demonology book out of her bag.

'Uh, Hel cat, do you know what you have here?'

'Yeah, a book on demons. Hopefully there is something to kill em... uhhh him. She was still sulking about Damien.

'Nooooo little witch, this is THE book on demons. Bound with the flesh of a witch and a demon, entrusted with the secrets and stories of both. It is seen as an integral part of the covenant between the two.' Lee spoke reverently, stroking its worn leather cover. This piqued Tessa's curiosity, finally giving him her full attention.

'You mean some sacred symbol of the witches and demons ended up shoved to the back shelves of the restricted section?' As Tessa spoke she began to regret her words, feeling the heat in the room rise. Lee's eyes snapped up, their anger creating a fire in their centre.

'WHAT? THEY DID WHAT TO THIS?' he shouted, not at Tessa, but to her. She was glad she never had to feel the heat from that temper front on, but she understood it.

'Yeah uhh... it was pretty dusty... but I guess it was safe.' She struggled to get the words out in the face of his anger and the stifling atmosphere of the room.

'They were entrusted to keep this according to its revered state. It contains rituals to keep the covenant strong and to keep the connection to Hel open,' Lee stated harshly, but he was beginning to calm. 'The Agency has lost its roots, disconnected from the old ways. It saddens me to see it.' he finished so defeatedly, withdrawing in on himself and cradling the book. Tessa moved to gently touch his face.

'I do not know what happened, nor why this book is where it was. But I am sure it will be looked after when I tell them I have found it.' She spoke quietly trying to console him.

'No, it shall not be left with them any longer. It cannot be. But that is a problem for another day. Yes, this book will have what we need to banish Berserk. Although it shall take some time to do so.' Tessa nodded at Lee's words, prepared for what was to come.

'What shall we do in the meantime?' Tessa tried to keep the conversation positive. Lee began to leaf through the ancient pages, many of them written in an arcane script.

'Here! This will help us for now. It will force him into the other planes of existence for a while and prevent him from coming back for a few hours. It will give us some time at least. I will have to get you to mix it for me though, lest I be sent there myself. The other planes are mighty boring when caught there.' Tessa stifled a giggle, sensing his wry admission was not something to be caught laughing at. She nodded before asking the question that was nagging at her.

'What is all this odd script?'

'That is the written language of all demon kind. We all must know it and learn it for our half of the magick in the world.' Tessa looked surprised, making Lee chuckle and continue.

'Yes, we too have our own magick, we may manipulate it through mantras of the old tongue, much like the witches' spells are of the old tongue. Didn't know that did you little witch?' Tessa shook her head silently, willing him to continue. 'I suppose that is one blessing that this book was neglected, witches no longer remember demon magick. They were supposed to be taught it as part of the balance, but some would gain far too much power. We have our own sigils also, ones we use and those which can be used against us. I do not know them all though and will have to research them. Hand me some paper so I can copy down what we need for this plane locking spell.' He requested in a distracted voice, his eyes fixed upon the book. Tessa sighed slightly, handing him the paper and guessing that was him entertained for the night.

She pulled out her laptop to write up the latest parts of her report and sent them in to the office before wandering into the kitchen in search of dinner.

Lee was still immersed in the book, scribbling down this and that. He had already given her the list, so as she grabbed out the ingredients for dinner, she also collected those for the spell.

Dinner was a fairly sombre affair, witch and demon both playing with their food and pushing it around their plates. Tessa had tried her hardest as a kitchen witch, putting all the magick and energy she could into the cooking, but that required actually eating the food. Neither were in the mood to eat, appetites thoroughly killed by Berserk.

After they had eaten, Tessa prepared a spell crafting area, this one would create a powder that must contact of the demon by being used on a weapon or introduced into a wound. Curiously enough it could also take effect by being blown into the eyes, something to do with tear ducts. The subversive nature of this spell and the reason for its need made Tessa on edge, she could be fired for this. The need to save Lee was greater than fear for her career right now, and that truly scared her.

An hour later Tessa was surrounded by half a dozen powder filled cloth bombs and her shoulders were aching from the effort. She quickly stashed them into her handbag for Berserk based emergencies. A zip-lock bag ensured that they wouldn't explode randomly with her favourite demon around. Lee could finally safely come back into the room now that the powder was gone, any residue blown into its component herbal parts by the fairly stiff breeze blowing through the window. He moved to close it then embraced Tessa, trying to stop her shivering. She gratefully returned the hug, she loathed the cold so.

Lee muttered something into her hair that Tessa could barely hear.

'What was that?' she asked, pulling away slightly to hear.

'Thank you. I know what this means to you, and I can't fathom why you would do it.' He spoke a little louder, still holding on to her tightly.

'I do this because I care about you Lee.' This time she extracted herself enough to see into his eyes and to steel herself for what she was going to say next. 'Hel, I love you.' She dropped her eyes as she said it, afraid to see his reaction. The first time she had said it after she interrupted the banishing spell meant to take him back to Hel, neither of them had acknowledged. This time there was no grand spell, no smoke and magick creating a storm around them.

He caught her chin and lifted her face until her eyes met his again then kissed her long and hard. When the ethers of the banishing spell had dissipated, Lee thought he had heard her admit to the love between them, but now she was saying it confidently, to his face.

'As I love you little witch. As I love you.' Tessa smiled as she felt her heart leap wildly, threatening to burst out of her chest. She threw herself back at him, knocking over her herb dish and shunting the coffee table as she went, but she barely noticed. Their lips met as he fell back onto the floor, smiling and kissing in a messy heap of limbs. Soon enough their clothes lay abandoned, their bodies entwined in that most intimate of fashions and the pleasure a game played between them. Tessa found delight in nipping Lee, flaring pains that made him buck and shift, pushing himself deeper every time she did. In turn Lee held her so tightly it was almost bruising, but any less and he could not thrust into her as thoroughly as he did, burying his entire shaft inside of her each time before nearly pulling out completely.

They continued long into the night, achieving orgasm again and again in celebration of their newly announced love. Much to Tessa's delight it seemed demons did not have a recovery time, at least not this one.

Chapter Eight

Needless to say, she had had very little rest the next day when she got up to return to the Agency, printing her reports and check if the medical records had arrived.

The scowl on Sir McAdams' face said it all. The area in front of his office was littered with archive boxes all marked as confidential. She really hadn't thought there would be that many male diabetics alive in Bayton, but she supposed that no one here really had a good diet, and many would be acquired diabetics. Tessa felt another headache brewing as she apologised to Sir McAdams, promising to have them moved as soon as she could.

His new secretary was absent today, so Tessa claimed her desk to begin searching through boxes. Luckily the law required all medical records to contain a picture of the patient at their last visit for identification purposes, so picking out the blondes was easy enough. Unfortunately, that wasn't something recorded on the computer system, hence searching for every male diabetic. She also excluded those who were too old or debilitated and was just beginning to read through the files of those she hadn't excluded when forensics called.

The search was again, a bust. There was no evidence to be found aside from this murderer also being right-handed and probably being the same as the last given the stylistic choices. Tessa thanked them and hung up feeling rather dejected, tapping idly on the secretary's computer.

Suddenly she had an odd thought, but one that may be worth a try. She turned on the computer and logged in before digging through her bag for her camera. Placing the card in the reader she opened up the internet for an image scan, entering the images of the murder. Four were rejected as no match before one had a hit. The convoluted design featuring an eye had a result that was uncannily similar. She saved that window, then another hit came, this time on some of the lettering carved into the body. Both pictures linked back to screen caps of some odd horror film Tessa had never heard of before, 'Denizens of Darkness'. The similarities were uncanny, and certainly not by luck. As she scanned through more pictures of the film she saw more and more of the murder carvings pop up. This sad little schlock horror had almost all of the more complex symbols present in their iconography, from supposedly arcane books to being embroidered into cloaks.

Feeling elated at the break while being utterly disgusted at what some people could watch, Tessa printed out a synopsis and review of the film and ordered it so she could watch it at home. Apparently, it was the tale of two murderous witches, a male and a female who killed people in order to... well that part was a little hazy, the reviewer actually wrote 'blah blah blah, take over the world, blah.' Little wonder it was so unpopular. It was the kind of film that gathered a cult like following. Tessa noted it down in her book and returned to reading the records, entering a list of names of all the eligible men into the Agency databases to see if any of them had offended in the past.

While she waited for that search to complete in the background, Tessa flicked over to a news webpage, to see what the press had dug up. Sometimes they could be better than Agency hunters at finding information. She was not, however, prepared for the headline that glared out at her.

WITCHES RESPONSIBLE FOR ANOTHER MAGICKAL MURDER, KILLS HUMAN IN EVIL RITUAL.

The editorial continued by stating this murder had been part of a 'spree' on humans, witches were to blame, and the Agency were trying to cover it up to protect their own kind.

Tessa reeled at the hate scrawled across the page, inciting humans to take arms and protect themselves against the evil of witches. They listed ways to kill this murderer of humans and those who aided them. Tessa sent a copy of the page to Sir McAdams to quash the story, but many had to have seen it in the three hours it had been up.

It had even been shared across many social sites, often with comments that made her sick to her stomach. She killed the window and closed her eyes, those incendiary words dancing across her mind, taunting her. She let her head fall into her hands, willing herself not to cry.

Her darkness was interrupted as the computer beeped quietly, indicating the search was done. There were a few dozen men who had been convicted and punished for a crime, not surprising considering it was Bayton, however Tessa narrowed it down to violent crimes only. This left only ten men, a far more palatable number than the boxes full. She kept her first list of eligible men as well as printing off this new list. Perhaps a little manual gumshoe work was called for, dropping in on each of the men to see what they were up to nowadays.

She tiredly turned off the computer and arranged for the boxes of copy records to be returned to the hospital for destruction. She kept only the boxes with her chosen few in. Checking her watch, Tessa was amazed to see that she had been working away for four hours, and as if on cue, her stomach growled viciously. On her way out to her car she called Lee to see if he wanted to meet her at the diner nearby for lunch. It was only a short drive over and Lee could use the planes to get there when she arrived.

Apparently to walk betwixt the planes of existence one must know intimately where they are going or have someone they knew well there, to act as a beacon. If not, they could become disorientated or overshoot their destination. An interesting concept given the consequences that may entail. It was entirely possible they could launch themselves into a wall, or spawn inside a human being.

They each ordered a burger and milkshake, the best to be found in the neighbourhood of the Agency headquarters. As an intern staying at the Agency she could never afford to eat here and had always longingly sniffed the amazing smell of food wafting over on the breeze, ripe with paprika and roasting meat.

Once again Lee had his horns hidden by the beanie, looking rather out of place in amongst the pompadours, shaven heads and mohawks. He grumbled about his hair as she excitedly tried to tell him about the film.

'Sounds stupid.' Lee grouchily whined as he threw last of his burger into his mouth. Tessa rolled her eyes.

'Yes, it's stupid, but it's where they are getting the ideas from for the supposed magickal murders.' She tried to reason with him, unwilling to lose the bliss of a full stomach.

'So I have to watch some crappy human movie that not even the humans like?' He was becoming downright belligerent, flicking a pickle slice onto the side of her drink. Tessa looked disgusted as she picked it off.

'No, you don't, you utter sack of misery, but I do, it may give us some clues. We don't have much else aside from visiting each of these guys on the list and politely asking them if they are killing people to incite some good ol' fashioned unrest. So yeah, I am gonna watch the stupid movie from start to finish and try to glean some damned insight from it. Is that all right with you, do I have your demonic permission? Because I don't particularly care if I don't. I just want to catch the stuffing murderer.' Tessa finished, feeling slightly winded from such a litany. Even Lee had the grace to look impressed at her efforts and gave her a break.

The diner had gotten oddly quiet, conversations had stopped in order to listen in, so Tessa decided to leave before she could shout more Agency secrets to a diner full of people. The car park was full of cars, but utterly devoid of people. It was just as well really, considering an obsidian horned demon was leaning casually against Tessa's car. Her hand immediately flew to her bag to grab hold of one of the little plane banishing bags while she tried to act nonchalant.

'Well, *witch*, I guess you lied to me. I wonder why you would do that for this pathetic demon? That really does annoy me, you know. I really cannot tolerate liars of any kind. What am I to do with you?' As Berserk spoke he menacingly dragged a blackened and pointed nail down the side of his face. Tessa shivered slightly but held her ground, Lee balling his hands into fists beside her. 'You know I can occasionally kill a witch or even a few humans if it means I get my target. I am not opposed to spilling some witch blood. Rather like it to be honest.'

'You will do nothing with her. You will do nothing but to return from whence you came, and rather swiftly at that.' Snarled Lee as he naturally fell into a far more archaic way of speaking. Berserk simply laughed, a large and very fake guffaw which seemed to be utterly devoid of any real warmth or humour.

'Or what Stanrael? Or what?'

Chapter Nine

The silence roared with the threats that lay between them, not needing to be spoken. The wind picked up, carrying distant voices and the usual city detritus. Tessa palmed a planes banishing ball and pulled off the sealing band.

'Just leave it alone Berserk. This has nothing to do with you.' Snapped Lee, trying to shield Tessa with his body.

'Well, I can't. See, I was summoned here for this purpose, and those who summoned me want results.' Answered Berserk, idly flexing his fists above some kind of concealed dagger Tessa only just noticed. She interrupted their little face off when she noticed what he had said, stepping forward to speak and see Beserk's face.

'Summoned? I thought you were normally sent out?'

'Nope, this time I got summoned. I guess you two pissed someone off!' guffawed Berserk again, enjoying the entire situation far too much for comfort. Tessa looked at Lee, horrified realisation in her eyes.

'It must have been Schimpf. He must have seen you that day at the store, and he is the only one who can do summonings. None of the other Agency hunters know about you or care.'

'Who cares people, make with the leaving Stanrael. I'm bored already.' Berserk interjected rudely. He was clearly used to people doing what he wanted them to do the first time he asked. Unfortunately for him, star-crossed lovers were notoriously difficult to convince.

Lee looked at him before drawing one of his odd serpentine blades from behind his back. Tessa swapped the plane banishing bag to her other hand and fished out her knife, ready herself. This simply widened the smile on Berserk's face as he drew his own dagger, which had an odd blade made from a blood red metal. There didn't seem to be any mundanes around luckily, a small blessing for the situation. The last thing they needed were any more headlines featuring violence.

Long moments passed again, then Berserk simply laughed one last time and launched himself toward them, with unbelievable speed. Lee stepped back in front of Tessa, blocking her off with his body again. Their daggers flashed as they got close enough, striking only metal again and again, never quite meeting flesh. The speed they moved was dizzying to Tessa, and now punches were thrown into the mix. There was the occasional thud as fist met flesh, however no blood had been drawn and neither demon was seeming to slow.

With both battling under such close proximity there was no way Tessa could get the powder for the planes spell in Berserk's face without also hitting Lee. If she did, they would probably just continue the fight in the other planes. Lee took a nasty blow to his jaw, however returned the favour by drawing the first blood and opening a large gash on Berserk's shoulder. Thinking as fast as she could and wanting to end the fight, Tessa shouted to Lee to look out and she threw the bag. Not at Berserk's face, but at the fresh wound on his arm. All it needed was the blood. The bag glanced off his neck but puffed out a spray of powder as it went, coating his upper arm. Berserk looked confused for a moment before it settled. The demon blurred then disappeared. Tessa ran over to Lee to make sure his face was free of powder, as well as checking him over for wounds. A killer bruise was already flourishing on his jaw and neck, but overall, he was well enough to put some distance between them and the planes locked hunter demon. They jumped into the car and took off, wheels squealing in their haste.

'I am going to kill Schimpf, that bloody little... weasel!' Tessa shouted from the adrenaline flooding her system, hitting the steering wheel as she drove. Lee remained quiet, brooding as he looked out of the window.

His odd mood continued when they returned home, and he cloistered himself in their bedroom with the Demonology book. Tessa left him to it, taking the hint that he wanted his solitude. Instead, she went around the apartment boosting the magickal protection she had and adding a few warding and hiding sigils. When she finally felt safe, Tessa drew the curtains and popped on the film her new pet murderer was emulating. It was exactly as awful as she thought it would be, full of clichés, bad acting and a few particularly brutal murder scenes. They were unfortunately identical to the ones going on in sunny Bayton, so Tessa called it in to the boss. Sir McAdams seemed positively thrilled by the prospect that a person was running loose and murdering people based on a D grade horror flick.

He also had the news that pressure was being put on them to wrap this one up fast, as the media was snowballing on the idea that there was magickal killing of mundanes occurring. As expected, this was causing a great deal of unrest. Several anti-magick groups were already stirring up the masses with a call for witch identification and 'control'. Tessa felt the pit of her stomach drop at the words, knowing exactly the kind of ideas they were advocating. There was still a lot of bad blood over the witch trials and genocides which had occurred throughout history, and that was before the world as a whole knew that witches existed.

After she finally got Sir McAdams off the phone, Tessa sat back and pondered her next move. The film was a big connection and may be able to be used with her list of ten names. She tried using a search engine and entered each of the names with the title of the film but came up with nothing. On a whim she began to search social media for the names as well as links or likes for the film. She was partway through the list when she fell asleep, the late nights finally catching up to her.

Chapter Ten

The morning was a black and pendulous one, storm clouds brewing over Bayton and rain threatening to wash some of the grime away. Tessa awoke in her own bed, Lee having carried her in there when he found her on the couch asleep. She felt much better, having had a full sleep before showering early and getting breakfast. The kettle had just about boiled for her morning tea when her phone blared the Agency emergency tone.

Tessa groaned loudly, turned off the kettle and grumbled all the way to her phone. A body had been found; an address was given and that was that. Sir McAdams wasn't even in yet; this order came from the night shift Lady in charge. Lee was still asleep, curled up with the cat, so Tessa left him a note with details of what had happened. As she walked to her car Tessa glared at the clouds, which were yet to unleash their burden.

The drive was short and sweet, ending up in another mundane dominated area of Bayton. A townhouse this time, the young resident a beautiful and promising medical student and much-loved local waitress. The attending police officers were all rather green looking, and at least one had lost their breakfast in the front garden by the look of the plants. Some bore chunks. The introductions were skipped in favour of a quick exchange of information and the promise of exchanged reports.

The front door had an odd eye with a pentacle in the place of an iris painted on it in blood, a disturbing greeting to the scene. Tessa took pictures and swabs for the forensic unit as rain started to patter down, just in case it washed away before they got there. She entered the little house tentatively, feeling rather like a sacrificial lamb. The poor girl had been killed in her main hall, by the looks of it she had been about to leave for the day. Her bag was flung to the side, study notes flowing out of it along with cosmetics and a purse. Tessa picked up the purse, discovering that one Clair O'Neal had not been robbed, her cash and bank cards were still present.

The stench that Tessa was beginning to consider a signature of the killer was present much stronger this time, testament to how soon they had found the girl. She supposed that a giant bloody eye tended to attract attention fast, even in Bayton. Once again, the walls were painted up and splattered with blood. Arcane lettering seemed to be taking form more and more in the sick graffiti, as well as the word curse mentioned a few times.

Tessa took in every pattern and detail, searching for sense or magick, but there was neither. The back of the door had a crass pentacle on it and chunks of congealed blood caked the handle. She also searched for fingerprints, but once again only found glove marks. Finally, Tessa looked to the body, needing to steady herself when she did.

While Clair had been beautiful in life, in death it was stolen from her. Lidless eyes stared up at her, the eyelids having been cut off, as her face had been defiled with cuts and gouges. Small stabs dotted under each eye to make her look even more unusual and her rich chestnut hair had been cut roughly. There were pieces of it around her body, however most of the hair seemed to have been taken.

Her body had been cut and stabbed repeatedly, mimicking the same patterns as the previous murders and the film. The monster doing this was obviously beginning to get creative, deferring from the film here and there and changing up the pattern. Tessa doubted that the eye or the pentacles were for any use but shock tactics. She suspected it would be mostly to give the media some extra hate fodder.

A theory was beginning to form in Tessa's mind that this was some kind of reverse hate crime, where the mundane killer was trying to frame those of a magickal nature for the murders, and would probably become more and more public about it. Whoever this was clearly hadn't made friends with sanity lately. Tessa finished looking over the body just as forensics arrived, with the same girl on the team as the last victim. Tessa nodded to her; glad she had someone in who knew the last scene. As they set up for their investigations, Tessa checked through the rest of the house, but nothing seemed out of place. Even the tiny courtyard was in perfect order, so she went back to watch the team working while she digested some of her thoughts.

They had already ruled out magickal involvement, as well as assessed that Clair O'Neal had only died approximately one hour earlier.

'She still be warm, see?' The forensics assistant offered the victim's hand to Tessa to check for herself, but she declined.

Tears sprang to her eyes when Tessa realised that just as she was waking up this beautiful girl had lost her life. Seeing so many bodies had already begun to weigh on her, she already dreamed of their faces at times. Tessa swiped her tears away stubbornly, determined to stop this particular brand of evil.

Suddenly the young forensics assistant ran over to her excitedly, clutching a zip lock bag in an outstretched arm. Tessa could barely get her to stop moving frenetically to be able to see the contents of the bag.

'Look Lady Bale, I found a hair, and it ain't one of the deadie's!' The forensics team leader cleared her throat angrily at the mention of the word 'deadie' and the assistant instantly looked horrified.

'Erm I means de-ceased, Lady Bale.' Tessa nodded, knowing it was more a matter of lexicon than disrespect for the dead. The bag did indeed contain a different hair, blonde with a twisty kink to it. It was definitely similar to the first one, and Tessa welcomed the extra evidence.

'Thanks, uhhh...' Tessa trailed off, realising she had no idea what her name was. Luckily the girl could take a hint.

'Amy... Amethyst,' she said brightly.

'Thanks Amy. By the way, I have some swabs from the front door, here,' replied Tessa, handing over a zip lock bag of her own. Amy took it and placed it with the other pile of evidence before going back to her work. Feeling like she wanted to be anywhere but here, Tessa took her leave, reminded that she had a score to settle with a certain slimy coworker back at the Agency.

It wasn't hard to find Schimpf, all Tessa needed to do was wander the halls of the Agency until she scented his particular stench. She swooped in on him dragging his scrawny body, limbs flailing, into one of the many alcoves present in the old building.

'What the shit Con-tessa? What is this?' he blustered, his face reddening rapidly. She had never confronted him this aggressively before, and he seemed both shocked and embarrassed.

'Like you didn't know I would come after when you invited the new friend out to play,' Tessa spat into his face. The look on Schimpf's face went from angry to confused in seconds, a response Tessa was not expecting. She had thought he would gloat, delight in the chaos and cruelty he had brought forth.

'What are you shitting on about? I am investigating the faery murders.'

'You summoned Berserk to take back Lee!' she cried, feeling close to exploding into tears. The confused looks continued.

'What? I don't know either of those names. What are you on about?' Schimpf looked at Tessa as if she had lost her mind completely.

'You saw Lee at the store and then... to get back at me... You had no idea did you?' Tessa finally conceded, a new horror dawning within her. If Schimpf hadn't brought up Berserk than who had? Now Mike Schimpf also knew Lee was still here as well, and could get her into some serious trouble.

'You mean that demon you had? The store? I didn't see anyone but your haughty ass, but now you tell me you stashed a demon here?' Tessa nodded, too horrified to respond. 'And this Berserk is what, a bounty hunter? You would risk that for the pretty boy demon? You know the enforcers can kill us right?' Schimpf asked, looking odd. Tessa nodded again.

'Not going to tease me for being useless or feminine for falling for my first demon? No bitter remarks or jabs?' Tessa muttered bitterly.

'Actually no. I uhhh know what it is like to be in... you know... l-l-love with someone. And have it taken away. But I promise you it wasn't me.' Tessa investigated Mike Schimpf's eyes, finding sincerity and even tears floating. He coughed and looked embarrassed, breaking the eye contact.

'Mike...' Was as far as she got before he interrupted her.

'Next time make sure you have your facts straight before you accost someone,' was his final gruff response before stepping back and stomping down the hallway. Tessa was left feeling utterly conflicted, and with the larger question of who had summoned Berserk.

She tottered out of the Agency feeling confused and a little silly. She highly doubted whoever was murdering the women in the case she was investigating had caught wind and had launched a pre-emptive attack, or was even capable of it. The only other person who had an interest in the matter was Damien, but he certainly didn't have the skills. Still, perhaps it was time to pay him a rather unfriendly visit.

Chapter Eleven

The night market was as busy as ever, the colder weather forcing people to huddle together around the fires in groups. It was cute and bonding in a slummy kind of way. People tended to share a lot more when forced together, whether it be an anecdote or just a cigarette. Tessa ducked past them all, snugly wrapped up in a furry leopard printed, silk lined coat that was the envy of more than one person there. She knocked on the little door that led to the rooms Damien kept, but as soon as it was answered by the usual heavy she bolted in, fearing the door would be slammed in her face.

The doorman may have been a muscled mountain, but he was slow and Tessa was halfway down the hallway before he had responded. Damien was on the phone when she found him, openly cringing when he saw her but didn't order her to be removed. He wrapped up the phone call quickly before looking at Tessa as if she was dirt on his pristine motorcycle.

'What do ye want?' He was offensively blunt.

'Glad to see you are still giving me the sweet nothings,' replied Tessa, already irked by his attitude.

'Ye come in 'ere just fer that? Scoot,' Damien snapped, flicking his lighter angrily. His hands fidgeted frantically, but at least he was not reaching for huis gun this time. This was the most dishevelled that Tessa had ever seen her former friend and flame. His mohawk had grown out in patchy stubble, his face was growing a ratty mess of hair that would look more appropriate further south. Even his clothes were dirty, stains littering a red bowling shirt and pants covered in grime.

Normally Damien dressed impeccably, but this was not the man Tessa once knew.

'Did you know Lee was here still? And do something about it?' She didn't bother dodging around the topic. Damien's mouth twisted at the mere mention of his name.

'Yeah I knew 'im demon was there. No one shits in this town without me gettin' the know-how,' spat Damien as he poured another drink, some cheap whisky straight. Previous Damien would never lower himself to drinking cheap whisky. 'The fucking demon be playin' happy houses, reckon it make'n me sick it does. So I gotten it dealt with. Done me a good deal too, they bin lookin for that demon, back where'n he came from.'

'What? Why? Why would you do that?' Tessa felt horrified.

'Like I said, makes me sick. Ain't natural like. Ye done traded me in for'n freak with horns. Woulda even bin better if it had bin 'nother guy. But ye ain't even got same species. But they gonna take the freak back.' Damien had an idly threatening gist to his words. Tessa couldn't come up with a response, she merely stood there as her mind tried to comprehend his anger. Finally, Damien motioned to the door guard, who began to herd her from the room. This stirred Tessa into action, and she began cussing and cursing at Damien as she was forced from the room.

Tessa was dumped rather ungraciously on the street, still angrily hurling abuse. When the steel door slammed shut, she finally conceded defeat, turning on her heel and stalking away through the market. Her old stall still had not been leased, ever since Tessa had killed the previous tenant. It stood empty, almost like a hollow shrine to what was.

Determined to make the outing worthwhile, Tessa went to see what was on offer at a few new magickal stalls, getting very excited at one seller who had excellent quality crow bone for sale as well as cat skulls and other bone items. The crow bone may help with a banishing spell powerful enough for Berserk, and she haggled furiously with the toothless seller in order to not get taken advantage of. Colourful piles of healing and magickal herbs lay at another stall, reminding Tessa of the beautiful images of India with mountains of spices. This was the side of Bayton that she loved.

Yes, it was a slum, but at the same time it was colourful, heady and wild. It called to her blood, begging her to immerse like some kind of wanderer queen. She, however, was no nomadic fantasy, she had a home and domestic bliss to get back to. With her crow bone in her bag, she finally decided to go home and break the news to Lee.

The cat, who was apparently now named Seti, was purring contentedly in Lee's lap when she closed the door and threw her bag down. She scratched it gently on the head as she relayed the sorry tale of the day to Lee. The soft fur was a welcome refuge from the anger within her, and she found herself appreciating that the cat had come to them.

'So after all that, it wasn't Schimpf. He was actually almost understanding and less creepy. I can't believe Damien would do that. Who knows what witch he has gotten onto the case?' she pondered aloud, sighing unhappily.

'A bloody strong one. To call up one as old and strong as Berserk you must either be personally very powerful, or you must be able to tap into the power of the Ley Lines, the Earth's magick. He really must have wanted me gone.' Lee looked so unhappy at that revelation that Tessa almost cried for him. Instead, she quietly gathered her strength before speaking.

'Well, we shall just have to fight our way out again. Did you find anything new from the book?'

'I did find a generic banishing spell, one that is powerful enough for him. But it needs not only crow bone but also a dog skull and nuummite. So not exactly stuff that is easy to find,' replied Lee. Slowly a hopeful smile grew across his face as she drew the crow bones from her bag. 'You do well little witch, you do well!' As he praised her, he pulled her into his arms. She welcomed the embrace, laying her head on his chest to hear his heartbeat and feel his warmth soak into her. Demons ran at a much higher temperature than humans, something Tessa was starting to get used to, along with the horns. She actually found them attractive now, something unique to the man she loved.

Tessa should have gotten up. She had so much to do, and there was still a murderer on the loose who needed to be dealt with. Somehow all of these urgencies faded away in the preciousness of these moments with Lee, simply curled in his arms.

They lay there, just touching and embracing until slowly the touches became more sensual and the kisses more urgent. The air itself changed, rapidly becoming more electric and heady. Tessa reached down to touch and tease the growing bulge in Lee's pants, to feel where he was straining against the zip, begging to be freed. She cheekily ran a finger up and down the covered length, delighting in the way he twitched and bucked at the lightest of touched. He watched her as she did, revelling at her beauty, the way the light illuminated her eyes, making them glow green.

Those eyes stared back at him, taking him in as urgently as a dehydrated man in the desert takes in the mirage of water. She needed this, she needed him. To feel safe, to feel sexy, to feel loved. Tessa slipped off her dress, clumsily pulling it over her head in her urgency. She kissed Lee on his lips, before trailing kisses down his chin, then his neck. With each button of his bowling shirt that Tessa undid, she trailed another kiss down his chest. She was almost at his waistline when her phone rang with the Agency emergency tone, loud and screeching. She paused a moment, weighing up whether she wanted to answer the call or keep going.

The moment didn't last long before she resumed her kiss trail, now unbuttoning and unzipping Lee's jeans. Tessa was about to take his length into his mouth to give a little oral stimulation when her phone went off again. Groaning loudly, she grabbed her phone off the table to answer it.

'Hello, Tess-' Was all she managed before she was interrupted.

'Lady Bale, it is Sir Gian from the evening shift, we have something here which I believe is from your case. We require you to come in and take a look.' Came the stiff reply. Sir Gian was a nice enough fellow, but he had a tendency to be too formal and was a very anachronistic person on the whole. He routinely wore suspenders and a formal waistcoat, highly polished shoes and a pocket square.

'Yes Sir, could you tell me any more about what it is?' Tessa asked calmly, trying not to show her annoyance.

'It appears to be some kind of voodoo item and has rather a lot of hair attached to it. According to the note it was sent to the Bayton Daily with, it is from Clair O'Neal.' Tessa cringed at the mention of Bayton's most widely read newspaper.

'Thank you Sir Gian, I will come in now.' Tessa waited for the reply before hanging up the phone, and was left holding a dead line. Sir Gian was not one to waste words. She hung up, rubbing her temples from frustration. Smiling wryly at Lee she sighed unhappily while he simply nodded. He poked out his bottom lip in a mock sulk.

'The Agency always gets to take you away from me... they get all the fun!' He was whining, but it matched the way Tessa felt.

'Trust me, this will not be fun. Something along the voodoo lines has shown up. Gotta go!' Tessa replied before kissing him and getting up.

Chapter Twelve

Tessa found the old front building of the Agency eerily deserted, having only a skeleton crew on for the night shift. She had to swipe a key-card to get in, and there was no cheerful receptionist to say hello with her classic dimpled smile. Even the interns had all returned to their dorms for the night.

She walked quickly through the halls, cringing at the way her heels echoed around her. Trying to remind herself that she was only creeping herself out, Tessa reached the final hall before her destination. The light from the main offices spilled out ahead of her, however her eye was suddenly caught by a light emanating from an open doorway to her right. It had an odd blue shade, and seemed to have a thick, almost soupy quality to it. Tessa stopped abruptly, oddly unable to walk on, just standing to attention. There she was frozen still, as the light grew brighter, before a feminine form burst forth from the doorway. She was beautiful and ethereal, with sad, empty eyes trailing tears as she glided along the floor. She wore a long dress which clung to her tiny, translucent shoulders and fell in waves to the floor. Their eyes met as the spirit of the woman passed in front of Tessa, stopping her dead. The lady in white even turned her ghostly head to look straight at Tessa, before continuing into and through the wall. As the last of the light faded Tessa could finally breathe again, then she was able to move.

Looking from the door to the wall and back again, Tessa tried to reconcile her mind with what she had just seen. Finally, all she could settle on was bolting the last few meters to the office. Sir Gian looked up in surprise when she burst through the door, the blood drained from her face.

'Lady Bale, what on Earth? What happened?' asked Sir Gian, without breaking his rhythm of correcting test papers from interns.

'A ghost! I saw a ghost in the hallway, a proper fucking translucent spirit!' shouted Tessa, causing a few other Agency busybodies to stick their heads into the room. A swift but stern glare from Sir Gian soon had them scurrying back to their respective areas.

'Lady Bale do not come in here spouting such profanity ever again. If you do so I shall have to have you written up. There are many things in this world Lady Bale, and we are well aware of the Lady in White. It appears that she must be of Agency stock, as all attempts at banishment have failed. An Agent must be prepared, not scared. Do you understand?' finished Sir Gian, actually stopping his corrections in order to admonish Tessa. She opened her mouth to argue the point but then thought the better of it. It was many months since she had been an intern, but Sir Gian's lessons still gave her a fear response.

'Yes, Sir Gian, please forgive me. You had something from my case please Sir?' She spoke humbly trying to appear contrite. It must have worked because his shoulders became less stiff, and his ever-present frown softened just a little.

'Lady Bale. As I mentioned on the telephone, it appears to be a voodoo item, and was sent in to the Bayton Daily along with a rather odd letter. The horrid newspaper has, of course, already started writing up the story and I believe have broken the news on the Internet. We are working on a quash order, but you know how these simple mundanes can be. Always looking for a sensationalised scandal.' He droned on, distain evident in the way the word mundane appeared to leave a bad taste in his mouth. Tessa tried not to cringe at him, knowing it was merely the attitude of witches at least 50 years ago talking.

Before magick had become accepted in mainstream society there had been a lot of secrecy and elitism amongst witches, for both safety and arrogance. They often considered themselves more evolved than the average mundane, a theory that had yet to be proven. Tessa simply nodded in response and picked up the letter and the 'voodoo item', pretending to be utterly engrossed in studying it.

On closer inspection it turned out to be just an ordinary poppet, the kind that Tessa herself used to sell at markets and others sold regularly. The chestnut hair taken from the corpse of Clair O'Neal had been roughly sewn onto its head and pins jabbed all over the tiny doll. The letter was written in a sprawling handwriting, so badly done that it took a few moments to decipher it.

'Dear Media.

I have used this voodoo doll to steal and seal in the soul of the girl I killed. I am collecting them all so I can have all the power of their pretty little souls, and I will sacrifice them so I can raise a demon. My demon will then cleanse Bayton of all humans, leaving witches only. His long claws will tear up women and children, and his cloven hooves will break the skulls of men. My first task was to kill the witch who was helping the humans, then to collect their souls. Finally, Bayton will be free of useless humans and then I will have all their souls to cleanse the world...'

Tessa looked up to Sir Gian as she read, raising her eyebrow sceptically. 'Sir, this is clearly utter bullsh... uh, lies. How can anyone honestly believe this?' As the query left her lips, she knew that this would be gleefully eaten up in the main population, eager to hate freely. For once Sir Gian broke his usual poise with a snort and a smirk.

'When stirred into fear of their life, people in general are rather willing to believe anything they are told.' Tessa shook her head sadly at his response and continued.

'I will only be happy when the world is clean and pure, with only magickal kind left. Then, my mission will be completed. It is one given to me by my spirits, and soon I will be in a magick only world.

Signed

The Soul Warlock'

Tessa turned the page over but there was nothing more. She fought the urge to laugh hysterically at the pathetic attempt to gain notoriety, as well as to throw a nasty light on to all magick users. She ran a hand over the poppet, but it remained inactivated and had certainly not been used to trap a soul. So now they were playing with red herrings, the type that could cause serious friction and possibly fragment the often-tenuous peace. However, the story had broken, and it was now up to the Agency to write up a press release against it. Then it was up to her to catch the ones behind the murders.

Tessa thanked Sir Gian before taking a few pictures and wrapping up the poppet and letter to take to forensics the next day. When it was safely stowed in her bag, she took her leave. Fear had her scuttling back through the passages as fast as her legs would take her. She kept her eyes firmly fixed on the floor in front of her, making sure to not look at any odd lights. She had almost made it back to her car in the nearly empty lot when the stench of sulphur caught her nose.

Her eyes darted around in panic, but she didn't see a demon until she was thrown against her car and slid down its side. Berserk followed her, using his huge body to corner her against it. Tessa felt bleary, having knocked her head in the fall, as well as at least bruising her ribs. Berserk shook her roughly before sticking his ugly face into hers, his breath reeking of sulphur.

'I don't appreciate the games witch. I don't like being stuffed around and I certainly don't bloody like being stuck in the other planes for two hours. Give me Stanrael or I will kill you here and now. Simple? Clear?' His voice was a vicious snarl, spit flying on her face with every word. Tessa fought the urge to wipe it off, instead she reached into her bag to feel for another banishing bomb. Despite the urgency, Tessa ensured her moves were nice and slow to avoid alerting him. She began to prattle to buy herself some time to search.

'I'm sorry, but he has been influencing me. I would never have fought back but he made me do it. He said it would be ok, and I must fight with him or else!' she pleaded, trying to widen her eyes as much as possible to feign innocence. All Tessa could feel in her bag was her bone handled knife, so she silently flicked it open.

'Or else what? What could that poor excuse of a demon possibly threaten you with that I can't beat?' Berserk actually giggled, clearly rather tickled by the very idea. Tessa saw this as her one and only moment, whipping the knife out of her bag and embedding it up to the hilt in his lower chest. The much larger demon fell back as she pushed him away from her and scrabbled in her bag for her keys. Praying it would start, she unlocked the door and jumped in.

Only when her engine had started and she was reversing out did Tessa look back to see what Berserk was doing. He had stood back up and was calmly watching her as she drove away, plucking the knife from his flesh. He seemed oddly amused for someone who now had blood pumping freely down his chest.

Chapter Thirteen

When she finally got home Tessa was greeted at the door by a very worried Lee, along with Seti twining around his ankles. Both of them seemed alarmed, the cat was even fluffy.

'What happened? I sensed you were having troubles with Berserk, but by the time I was ready the urgency had already gone.' Lee almost shouted while lifting limbs to inspect for injuries. Tessa shook her head slowly, still too scared and tired to think. Satisfied that the blood present wasn't hers, Lee guided her over to the couch and settled her down.

For long moments Tessa just wanted to sit in Lee's arms, just to absorb their warmth and feel safe. Eventually she stopped shaking and calmed down enough to open up.

'Berserk was waiting for me when I left the Agency, I am sure of it. He was threatening me, asking where you were, I couldn't find any of those stupid balls, so I just had my knife and I... I stabbed him. I had to! Then I got away, I looked back, and he seemed fine. But there was blood everywhere, I am sure I hit his heart like I was trained to. But he was just smiling at me. Now he has my knife too, I gave him a weapon,' blurted Tessa, feeling guilty about losing her weapon to the enemy. She allowed a few tears to fall as she spoke, trying not to break down completely. Lee wiped them away with a tender touch.

'That demon does not need weapons, in fact, he spurns them completely. You certainly don't need to worry about that aspect. He is a weapon. He likes to simply crush his opponents. Plus, have some logic darling, he is a part of this world as much as you or I, he can get his own weapons.' Lee comforted her with his rational words.

Tessa had known that, but somehow having it said to her made all the difference. Finally, she felt her heart rate began to slow and her hysteria decreased for the first time since the attack. She took the opportunity to stay in his arms and get some well needed attention. It helped her ignore the world for a little while. In those arms there were no gruesome murders awaiting her, nor were there blood lusting, head crushing demons. Lee held her as long as she wanted, and it was rather late by the time they decided to go to bed.

The next morning dawned bright and early, sunlight glaring into Tessa's eyes and forcing her to wake. Usually her curtains were tightly closed, Tessa abhorred the sunlight in the morning. As she struggled to see she wondered if she had been that tired that she had forgotten to draw the curtains. The realisation that she had never opened them hit her like a bullet train. She sat bolt upright, her eyes darting around the room.

Scarred into the wall was a threat that made Tessa's heart stop. Scrawled on the wall in front of her was simply the words 'FOUND YOU! PEEKABOO!' Stabbed into the wall was her knife, with blood still coating the hilt. She hit Lee to wake him up, still paralysed from fear. He roused with a shout, then fell into a horrified silence as Tessa pointed out the bloody graffiti.

Lee jumped out of bed and ran through the apartment, searching every hiding place to see if Berserk was waiting to jump out and slaughter them both. When Lee was satisfied that Berserk had left, he returned to the bedroom to check on Tessa. She was sitting clutching Seti to her chest, and to the cat's credit, he was taking it. His eyes were pulled wide open from her frantically petting hand. Her eyes hadn't moved from the blood, and she rocked on the spot slightly.

Quietly Lee fetched a wash cloth and began to scrub off the blood, the coppery scent confirming its origin. Unfortunately the message itself was still carved into the wall, courtesy of her knife. When the wall was as clean as he could make it, he sat down beside her and took her into his arms. They sat in a shocked silence, all three of them, until Tessa finally broke it.

'Why didn't he just do it then and there? Why play with us like this?' She begged Lee for a logic that did not exist.

'Because he is utterly sick and I am sure he is loving being free from Hel for a while. He likes to play with his prey and make them suffer for his enjoyment. It's why he hasn't made a major attack, he wants to give us time to make some plan to defeat him, then he will have a challenge,' Lee replied, his voice twisted with wry bitterness. They were dealing with twisted mind in charge of a weapon of a body. He was of a mind to turn himself in to save Tessa, but she quickly put a stop to that idea as soon as he voiced it.

'Don't you dare! I love you and I am here to fight this one with you. We need to take a serious look at that book. It must have a way to defeat him.' She was starting to feel her fight coming back and she was downright pissed off now that he had dared to enter and defile her home. She looked at him earnestly, her green eyes boring into his with all of her love and stubbornness shining forth. Lee felt himself giving in, unable to resist her earnest nature.

'Deal, but we stay at a motel or something until we are done with it all ok?' Tessa nodded back at him, seeing the sense in such a request.

Now that the message was almost gone and the house checked over, Tessa finally felt confident enough to take a shower and get ready for the day. She had to run the poppet and letter over to the forensic department at the Agency, and wanted to do so as soon as she could. She had also contacted Susan to say she had found the ring, and the girl was keen to collect it. Lee had wanted to accompany and protect her, but Tessa insisted that he stay home and research how to deal with Berserk. She even gave him access to her computer in case the Internet had something to offer.

The drive over to the Agency was short and uneventful, just the way Tessa liked it. As soon as she entered the building she was reminded of her ghostly interaction of the night before. In all the terror of the previous night and morning, she had completely forgotten about it, now she couldn't help but be reminded. The sun was blazing in and Tessa could feel very little around her on the magickal spectrum, so she confidently walked the halls.

At one point she could have sworn she smelled the eau d'Schimpf, but hurried footsteps in the other direction had left the adjoining passageway empty. It seemed he had gone from hassling her to avoiding her.

Forensics dubiously took the poppet and letter, dusting it then and there so Tessa could see there were no fingerprints. She left them to process the rest as she had a burning question to ask Lady Kirk.

Her rooms were as sweet smelling as ever, however the Lady herself was crankily scolding another hunter over a screwed up order. Tessa took one look at the anger on her face and decided to give it a miss. Instead she headed over to talk to Sir McAdams in his office. He looked simply delighted to see her.

'Lady Bale, what good timing. I had just sent you the latest collection of press reports on the 'Soul Collector'. The director has requested that we do a press junket together to put this idea to rest. While I say requested, we both know what it really means. We have been given until tomorrow morning to collect our information, then we go in front of the pack from 10:30am. Now, you are definitely sure this is non magickal?' It was more of a demand than a question, his face becoming a blotchy red as he spoke. Tessa nodded in reply.

'Yep, there is no magick attached at all to any of the victims, and that poppet was a generic one and inactivated.' Sir McAdams raised an eyebrow at her words.

'Poppet?' he questioned flatly. The man was stressed.

'Uh the one received yesterday evening... with the soul collecting powers apparently.' Tessa was beginning to feel very awkward about this turn of conversation. As her supervisor, Sir McAdams should have been the first to know.

'I don't know about any of this, I thought the media was just stirring things up again. What?'

'Well this poppet with the hair of Clair O'Neal sewn onto it was sent to the Bayton Daily, along with this utterly nutbag letter saying that this idiot would collect souls and destroy all the 'humans' eventually. It was pathetic, but clearly people went for it. I was called in by Sir Gian, who-'

'That prick? Thats why I didn't get told about any of this. I am surprised he even told you given his grudge against me. He tends to include those who work for me in his stupid vendetta. Useless ars... uh well that explains that then.' Sir McAdams was now huffing and puffing in his efforts to stay calm. This was the first time Tessa had heard about any rivalry between them and was rather curious. She didn't speak, trying to encourage him to continue. 'So apparently they now think he is legitimately collecting souls? Jeez, this is going to be a fun press hustle. No wonder they are loving the story. Did you know that there is already a local political party lobbying for a registry of magickal practitioners and sequestration of the populations? Oh, and there is a great big stinking 'Save the Humans' protest. Whatever this asshole wants, he is doing it well,' grumbled Sir McAdams, as Tessa numbed out in shock.

While there had always been the little jibes and occasional bigot, this was a full-scale attack. There was something so organised about it all that made Tessa's intuition shudder. This was hatred and fear mongering, to end in what? A genocide? Various scenarios ticked through Tessa's mind as she continued to stare at Sir McAdams, utterly dumbfounded.

'Well, I hope you don't just sit and stare like that tomorrow. It's all a scary idea, but this is why we need to get out there and talk about it tomorrow. We have to try and talk these idiots down. Are we any closer to an answer on who it is yet?' The question was surprisingly patiently presented. Given that he was back to constantly trying to get a glimpse down Tessa's top, she wasn't too surprised that he was being accommodating.

'It's a male, blonde hair with a kink to it, diabetic, stinky. An all-round great chap. Apparently only targets women. The letter stated he killed Stacia Sing because she helped 'humans' and the rest were just because they were mundanes. He definitely seems intent in stirring up some hatred and bigotry by essentially framing magickal types as murderous power freaks. I was running a search for male diabetics with a criminal record, but so far nothing promising has popped up. Most are in jail, have left Bayton or aren't blonde. Oh and a few are dead it seems.' Tessa ticked each point off on her fingers as she spoke. Sir McAdams snorted slightly at the description.

'You have the medical records, yes? There was certainly enough clogging up my office. What about checking for those with a psych history, perhaps something to do with a traumatic event involving magick or the like. Classic weird shit. Sounds like this little idiot doesn't get out much. Especially with that weird movie shit.'

'I forgot about that. Need to look into that too. It was a terrible film. What a waste of celluloid,' Tessa quipped, making Sir McAdams snort and then burst into laughter. Tessa was starting to appreciate working with the Sir, finding this an almost pleasant conversation. As tears began to run down his face, his laughter subsided, and he could eventually speak in a wheeze.

'Ok well it sounds like you have plenty to go on. Please research as much as possible before tomorrow. I will meet you here at say... 10? Then we can prepare a bit before we get thrown to the wolves. I will see you then,' he finished, giving her a good solid leer followed by a long look up and down her body as Tessa stood up. *Scratch that, he was clearly still a complete pervert*, thought Tessa bitterly as she caught the look.

As Tessa rose to leave Sir McAdams' phone shrilled loudly and she heard him answer. She was just shouldering her bag when he covered the receiver.

'Wait!' he snapped as he went back to listening to someone who spoke a mile a minute. He scribbled something onto the corner of a piece of paper which he tore off and pushed across the table. On the scrap was an address, a park in North Bayton which was popular for weddings and drug deals if Tessa remembered correctly. Sir McAdams was nodding and giving a curt *yes* every now and then.

As Tessa sat there she clicked her immaculate nails, waiting for him to finish. She was speculating wildly as to what was being said, ranging from a new murder to some kind of place to investigate. Judging by the look on Sir McAdams' face, it was another murder. She made a stabby-stabby motion in the air. He nodded in response, pointing to the address. Whoever was on the other end of the phone was clearly still in full swing so Sir McAdams waved her out, indicating that he would message her the details. Tessa nodded, rolled her eyes and grabbed the slip of paper.

While driving over to the park she called Lee to update him about where she was going. Tessa's stomach roiled angrily, nerves about such a public murder made her feel positively nauseated. The beep of her phone when the promised message came in made her jump. Nikita Rouse had already been identified as the victim which was fast but not surprising given that she had a famous stage show as Nikita LaRouge. She was a burlesque dancer and model, good enough to be able to make it a full-time gig. Now Tessa understood why her body was left in such a public place.

With Nikita being a local celebrity the news would travel like wild fire and there was no way the Agency could quash it. The bastard was getting brash.

Susan's ring would have to wait.

Chapter Fourteen

There was the usual cluster of gawkers in the park, all jostling to get the best view of the body. Tessa parked as close as she could without running over the people in the group who all refused to move. The mundane police officers who were charged with minding the body stood shivering in the public glare. They were clearly unhappy to be left alone with the body and a curious crowd, and Tessa could see why. Nikita had always been small, but now her body looked utterly frail and broken.

Her limbs stuck out at odd angles and her famous natural auburn hair was matted with blood. Her deep blue eyes glared out of her face; the lids cut away viciously. Her pale skin was bruised and cut up, a multitude of cuts criss-crossing her face in a series of Xs. Her body had all the usual symbols carved into it, the eyes, pentagrams and arcane runes. He had really outdone himself this time however, using her blood to paint a huge tetragrammaton underneath her body. The crowd oohed as each detail was noted, photographed and recorded. When she began to closely inspect the details of Nikita Rouse, Tessa noticed an odd bruising around her mouth along with an abnormal shape of her lips. She parted them gently, retching loudly at what she saw.

The poor girl had undergone yet another torture, each of her teeth had been pulled out or broken in the process. Given the amount of bruising and blood in her mouth Tessa could safely guess that they had been pulled before she had died. Feeling a lump in her throat, Tessa fought to not cry, her empathy for what Nikita had undergone beginning to overwhelm her. As she paused, she heard the whispered comments from her dirty little audience. Titters about the evils of magick and banning witches were filtering into her ears, distracting her from the work to be done. Tessa looked up sharply, but none would meet her gaze. She looked at each and every person gathered until everyone fell silent, except for one insidious voice.

A male voice over the back of the crowd whispered about vigilante justice and destruction of the freaks, but Tessa could not place who it was. She indicated for the people in front of her to move, but the voice stopped when they shuffled aside. She searched the dirty faces before her until she saw something she barely believed. Her heart leapt when she saw a pale face and blonde frizzy hair on a man in sunglasses and a long coat, but he was already turning and running away.

Tessa pushed through the remaining people as she pulled her phone out of her bag, hitting the speed dial to Sir McAdams' office. She thanked her lucky stars that she had chosen to wear her boots today as she broke into a full run. Luckily she was yet to dismiss the other police officers present, and she hoped they would control the scene.

'Tessa, what have you found?' Drawled Sir McAdams, sounding as if he had all day, although that was probably only because Tessa was in such a hurry.

'Sir, I have spotted a suspect who ran from me. He matches the description and is running down Dunnear Ramble. I might need some help here.' Tessa shouted into the phone, only slightly beginning to pant from the exertion. For whole seconds there was silence down the line as the Sir realised the importance of what Tessa was saying.

'Right Lady Bale, I will run a call out, hold on...' The phone was muffled as Sir McAdams made the call on his mobile. The man with the kinky hair turned left, Tessa making the corner not long after. The smelly diabetic must have also been unfit as she was gaining on him rapidly.

'Tessa, we have another Agent a minute away, keep calling the streets and I will pass them on. I am also...'

'We have turned onto Bourke Avenue Sir.' More muffled noises passed her message along as the man turned another corner, slamming his shoulder into a pole as he went. A sickening crack rang out, but he kept running, further into the industrial area of North Bayton.

'I think it said Darwin Street Sir!' Tessa became more breathy as she was beginning to tire. The man was close enough that Tessa could smell the distinct stench of the unwashed, with that acrid fruity tang of keto acidosis. The fact that he was sweating certainly didn't help, making the odour almost overwhelming as Tessa gulped for air.

'I am also mobilising a tactical unit to enter the area and attempt to surround him, they will arrive in four minutes. Miles should be there in seconds in an Agency vehicle.' The man ahead disappeared around another corner, this time entering a small alley off Darwin Street. Tessa launched herself around it after him in time to see the ends of his coat trailing around another turn.

'Sir, we have entered an alley, it's a maze here Sir. We are still travelling roughly north east. Suspect is wearing a black trench coat.' She was gasping by now, entering the next alley only to see a warehouse door fluttering on the breeze. She pushed it open carefully while whispering her location into the phone, digging another knife out of her back pocket as she did. She stole into the room, eyes straining against the dark of the indoor area. Every small window was covered in grime, making the inside of the warehouse almost pitch black.

As the sun spots began to fade, she realised she was alone in the huge expanse of the warehouse. There was no movement at all aside from the dust flurries that were beginning to settle.

In the distance she heard the familiar bleep siren of the Agency emergency vehicles, echoing around the tin building. Tessa looked all around the floor and walls, even pulling out a torch to search for any kind of trail. She jumped when an odd voice shouted at her until Tessa realised that she was still on the call to Sir McAdams.

'Goddamn it Bale, what is going on? Are you ok?' Screamed the speaker, shattering the silence within the warehouse. Tessa flinched as she put the phone to her ear.

'Yes Sir, sorry Sir. I entered a warehouse off the alley, but he was gone. He knew the area well; I think he must have a bolt hole nearby as there is no sign of him. Where was that search team?' Tessa asked, hoping he wouldn't be too angry with her for losing the suspect. He huffed and puffed, clearly out of breath from the exertion of shouting and raising the cavalry from the comfort of his own desk.

'They are on Darwin Street, apparently it has many alleyways. Damned fools aren't game to look down each of them until you come out and show them the way. Can you find your way back?' His voice was a monotone drone when he finally caught his breath. Tessa took another look around the warehouse and shrugged.

'Yeah, there isn't much else I can do here... guess I can go get them. I will call again when I know more.' Tessa said before hanging up. She looked around the room one last time, noting a slight smell of sulphur, before turning to leave. A spray of pain suddenly radiated across the back of her head, and she fell forward. The last of her consciousness was spent watching her phone crunched under a boot before she was dragged off the dusty floor.

Chapter Fifteen

C onsciousness eluded Tessa, every time she thought she had a grasp on it, she slipped away again. Dreams and waking moments merged until she wasn't sure which was which. All she knew was pain and despair, a torture that was both physical and mental. Finally, she managed to rouse enough to get an idea of what her environment was like, although all that met her gaze was stone, moss and water. Her vision was still too constrained to see any further than that. The darkness was beginning to settle again when Tessa was kicked in the ribs, feeling at least one snap under the pressure of a massive boot and making her gasp.

'Wake up. I need you conscious to bring *him* here.' A vicious voice hissed in her ear. It seemed familiar, but Tessa was too groggy to really place it. She tried to speak but could only groan in response. 'That's better. It's not your lucky day I'm afraid. I wanted to play, really have some fun, you know? But the powers that be seem to be desperate to get things sorted out, so no more play. Stanrael dies today, witch.' The voice and the context sparked in her brain, as Tessa's memory fell into place. She looked up to see the blurry outline of Berserk, a hulking mass clothed in black. Tessa was glad she couldn't actually see his face, but she could imagine the expression all the same.

'Why... why I here?' she rasped, her lungs screaming with the effort. He laughed. He actually *laughed* at her confusion and agony.

'You are rather stupid for a witch, aren't you? You being in a threatening situation will call Stanrael right here, the blood bond is tight between you, especially as you have clearly shared other bodily fluids. I just have to...' With that he lashed out, bringing a boot down on her arm before kicking her in the face. Her nose shattered instantly, filling her mouth and sinuses with blood. The urge to scream tore her up inside, but she kept it in, refusing to let him see her pain. Sweet darkness rose again, and Tessa welcomed it's embrace. *Why was it always her nose?*

'Goddamn you, I told you to stay awake. It's been hours and Stanrael still hasn't shown. WAKE UP!' Berserk was screaming at Tessa now, his sharp voice invading her sweet repose from reality. Tessa moved her head slowly, gasping in pain as she felt her ribs shift with the movement. The floor was slick with blood from her nose, which seemed to have stopped bleeding at some time when she was passed out.

Her eyesight slowly came into focus, at last she could see where she was. Stone walls towered around her, all damp and coated with moss. Tree branches jutted in at some places, and as she stretched to look up, Tessa realised there was no roof, only more branches and a dusky sky. Realising how long she had been here, Tessa felt a panic begin to rise within her. It had gotten to nightfall, and she was missing. Surely they knew there was something severely wrong with her disappearance now?

Berserk was leaning against one of the cobbled walls, smirking at his handiwork. Tessa looked over to him wishing death upon him and all his ancestors.

'Well witch, now you're finally back with us that pathetic excuse for a demon may show his face. But then again, he may not. Perhaps he doesn't love you enough to risk this little adventure and return to Hel. Now wouldn't that be funny? I would have to hunt him of course, but in the meantime, I would have a pet witch to play with.' His grin widened as he looked her up and down, leering at every point her clothes were torn and bruised flesh was revealed.

The idea of being violated spawned pure horror in Tessa, her mind frozen in fear. This truly was her nightmare, a lifelong fear come to fruition before her eyes. She looked up at Berserk, but her eye was drawn to an area to his left, where it looked as if the air itself was bending oddly. Sulphur pervaded the air, and Berserk cracked a smile.

'Finally he ar-' He was cut off as Lee burst from the shimmering air and threw himself at the enforcer, tackling him into the wall. Taken off guard, Berserk was thrown against the stone, hitting his head and slumping to the floor. Lee pulled himself free from the stunned demon and ran over to Tessa.

'Tess, darling, are you ok? Here, it's the banishing spell, we just need the blood of a witch and her to do the incantation.' Tessa nodded weakly, holding out a hand to grab the tiny vial. Lee looked as if he was about to force her to let him do it, but Berserk chose that moment to retaliate with a tackle of his own. The vial was knocked out of Lee's hand as he was propelled forward, landing on the stone floor heavily. It flew through the air and, ignoring the pain which blazed through her ribs, Tessa threw herself towards it. She watched in absolute horror as it smashed on the stone floor, sending glass and powdered herbs everywhere. Time seemed to slow all around her, the world narrowing down to one tiny vial that had contained her hope.

Tessa looked up to Lee, who was grappling with Berserk on the floor. He hadn't yet noticed what had happened. Berserk must have gotten some hits in as Lee bore several rapidly swelling red marks to his arms and face. The enforcer had a split lip and what looked to be a shattered cheekbone, but he clearly had the upper hand. Lee was now pinned beneath him, the older demon using his bulk to incapacitate him while he attempted to strangle him with one hand, the other still landing hits. Tessa could tell that Lee was struggling, the time taken to check up on her causing him to lose his advantage and the fight.

Lee was going to die, and Tessa could only sit by and watch. She felt a tear crest then begin to roll down her face, futility making her almost hysterical. Lee was retaliating slower and slower, his eyes half shut and bleary. He looked over to Tessa, a glance with pure finality and love. She looked around, desperate for any kind of weapon, until her eyes settled again on the shattered vial. Praying to all and sundry, Tessa slapped her hand down onto the broken glass and herbs, barely feeling the pain as it cut into her skin. The blood from her hand instantly mixed with the herbs and became tacky, so she closed her fist around as much of it as possible and began to drag her body over to the two demons.

They hadn't even noticed her actions in their battle to destroy the other, so hell bent on it. Tessa inched closer as Lee's eyelids began to flutter, she screamed his name as she brought her hand down on Berserk's back, leaving a wide trail of gluggy blood. Lee roused enough to make eye contact.

'Incantation?' shouted Tessa as Berserk threw her off him and sent her skidding across the floor. Initially Lee could only manage a slight gasp, but he cleared his throat and tried again.

'Expelle daemonem coercitor in potestate terrae matris.' Berserk stopped moving, a sneer on his face as he laughed loudly. Tessa drew on every ounce of power she had before she opened up to the Earth, feeling deep into it for the power of the Mother. A ley line answered the call, filling her with a shimmering magick, with a wildness that threatened to overwhelm her.

'Expelle daemonem coercitor in potestate terrae matris!' She wailed desperately, feeling the Earth magick overflow and flood the room around her. The words gave way to a simple scream of power, Tessa hoping beyond hope that there was enough of each of the herbs in the mix on Berserk to respond to all this power.

For a second, nothing happened, they were simply bathed in an overwhelming amount of power, but a second later the mix activated, and light shone forth. The sneer on Berserk's face turned to confusion and then anger when he had realised what had happened. Light overwhelmed him, first as an aura, then his entire being turned to light. It became so bright that Tessa had to shy away from it. A smell of sulphur sharply rose, making her gag and shooting pain through her injured nose. As quickly as it rose it was gone, leaving sunspots on her vision and them alone in the room.

Chapter Sixteen

Tessa slumped to the floor beside Lee, who lay prone with his eyes closed. She reached out a hand to gently touch his face, fearing the worst. Seconds passed, feeling like years to Tessa, but slowly his eyelids began to flicker as he came to. She breathed a long sigh of relief and pulled herself closer to cradle his head.

'Well he is gone my love, I am so sorry it took me so long... if you... it will be my fault.' Tears began to fall down her face as Lee began to stir more, clearly upset at what Tessa was saying. He began to slowly shake his head. 'It's true. And now I don't know how we are going to get out of here. It's so cold... I'm so tired. We are going to die here. I can't walk myself, let alone carry you. No one knows where we are.'

Lee began to shake his head again, easing something out of his pocket. It was a tracker, with a beautiful red flashing light.

'A-gen-cy,' rasped Lee, smiling up at Tessa as best he could. One whole side of his face was unable to move. She couldn't believe it. They were saved but had survived the battle to lose the war.

Now that the Agency knew she would surely lose her job, and Lee would be sent back to Hel. The worries ran through her mind as her head began to sink, the exhaustion and pain finally catching up to her.

Lights began to flash over her eyes; muffled voices and the smell of disinfectant began to overwhelm Tessa as she ducked in and out of consciousness. She was vaguely aware of being moved again and again, being poked and prodded and plenty of pain. Passing out again was a sweet relief, but it didn't last long.

The room was quiet when Tessa woke and could finally force her eyes open, the dim light only slightly painful. It took a few moments of blinking for her blurry vision to clear, but she was clearly in some kind of hospital. She could have cried with relief when she realised the rocky dungeon was gone. The room was fairly empty, that normal soft blue of an Agency hospital room. Tessa strained her neck to see if she could view the other bed in the room, but it appeared empty.

Next, she tried to take stock of her injuries, but she just ached all over. She was about to start fussing with the bandages when an annoyingly smiley nurse walked in.

'Well, she lives! How are you doing dear?' she asked inanely, her smile revealing crooked teeth and dimples. Tessa decided then and there that she hated dimples.

'D- ow... dandy,' quipped Tessa, cringing at the pain talking brought her. The chipper nurse grinned at her before beginning to look her over, checking various monitors and her IV lines. When she had finished and noted down her findings she left, beckoning for someone else to enter. Sir McAdams hulked into the room, his face darkened with anger.

'Contessa Bale, do you have any idea of the mess you are in?' His voice was sterner than Tessa thought he was capable of. She looked guilty as sin, shaking her head as her heart sank.

'You have broken both our rules and the law, kept this demon around and jeopardised a mission to do so. The consequences for this may be very far reaching.'

'Sir, I... I don't know what to say. I just... it's love Sir,' Tessa stammered, trying to think of the right thing to say, but finding nothing. Sir McAdams sighed loudly, making Tessa flinch in the face of his disappointment.

'Honestly, off the record Contessa, I am jealous as Hel. I have never had someone do that for me or cared enough about someone to do it for. It takes guts.' Tessa sat silently, scarcely believing her ears. She didn't want to speak and interrupt what he was building up to. 'When that demon contacted me, I didn't know what to think, you had already been gone so long. But I gave him some time. Glad I did now. He managed to find you when we were still at a loss as to what had even happened to you. The warehouse was deserted, and the task force searched the area but found nothing of you or the case. So, the big fella wanders into the Agency looking for me and we did a deal,' finished Sir McAdams with a knowing smile. Suspicion and curiosity warred within Tessa to be the greater emotion. The mention of a deal, with that smile, was unsettling. She had a feeling that they were now trapped.

'A deal? Which was?' Tessa chose her words cautiously.

'I give him the spell to defeat the enforcer if he saves my most promising young hunter amongst other things. It was simple really,' replied the Sir, puffing out his chest with his own sense of self satisfaction. Tessa smiled and settled back into the pillows a little easier now. The 'other things' concerned her, but right now she wasn't willing to look the gift horse in the mouth.

'So, he is... alive?'

'Yes, alive and being healed as we speak. You are both being put on accelerated healing due to the case. The task force who picked you up was sent out under the guise that this was related to the case, not a rogue demon. So now we need to patch you up and get it solved before people ask questions.' Tessa nodded emphatically, prepared to do anything to keep Lee safe and out of Hel. The motion flared her headache and she winced in pain.

'You will try anything to get out of a press conference, won't you?' Joked Sir McAdams gruffly. Tessa smiled weakly in response.

'You know it.' The cocky response was choked out before breaking into a painful coughing fit. When it ceased, she could finally continue. 'How did that work out?' This time it was Sir McAdams' turn to wince.

'They ate us alive. Despite the litany of evidence I presented, it was a runaway train. There is already a draft bill being written up to either contain or ban magick, probably along with its users. Soon it will be lynch mobs in the street with flaming brands.' Sir McAdams finished with a loud sigh of despondence. Tessa had never seen her boss like this before.

'We will get this sorted out Sir, I promise.' She spoke confidently, stifling the urge to wince again at the effort. Her bravado must have paid off as he nodded, at first slowly and then more assertively.

'Yes, we shall. While you are in here could you please write up a case report for me of everything so far? I shall forward it to Elder Jacksom, who is overseeing all the cases currently being investigated. She is eager to see how far we have gotten, given that political puppets are now involved. I suspect... no, never mind. You focus on getting better.' He clearly meant to say something, but took it back at the last second. She caught him helping himself to a leer of her in her hospital gown as he left. Tessa smiled at his smarmy reliability and settled back for another sleep.

Chapter Seventeen

The report she had typed and sent on her hand-held tablet had taken Tessa hours to write in between sleeps and healing sessions, but by the end of the day she was already up on her feet. The need to escape the nurses and sneak in to see her spunky demon may have had a lot to do with it. He was in the room across the hall from hers and had undergone a battery of healing sessions himself.

His face was still sallow and dark bags hung under his eyes, but Lee looked utterly perfect to Tessa. She eased herself into a chair by his bed so as not to wake him, then took his hand gently.

The healers found her sleeping sitting in the chair with her head resting on the bed. She was still clutching Lee's hand. They shooed her back to her own room to heal, but gave up after Tessa was found back by his side another three times. By that stage all she had left was her extensive bruising, while Lee still had a few broken bones to fix.

When she was finally able to leave the healing centre, she jumped at the chance. She kissed Lee gently on the head before she left, hoping he would understand. It would only be a short trip out, but Tessa had a darkness and an anger in her that was begging to be released.

Tessa took a taxi to the market place, deserted during the day aside from a few dirty kids playing in the dust while their parents did all manner of deals in the alleys. The door to Damien's rooms was answered as quickly as ever, the usual stupid slab of man protecting the hall beyond.

'Uhrrr Dame don't want no vis'ters.'

'Tough, he is getting one. And he damn well will see me. Tell the pissant to come on out here.' Tessa tapped a toe on the floor impatiently while the doorman clearly wrestled with conflicting thoughts about what he should do.

'Uhrrr Dame don't want.' He began to say, but Tessa held up a hand to silence him.

'Ok shut up you big lug and go and get that shit head out of his rat hole,' stated Tessa, raising her voice for extra effect. Meaty moved to comply, but Damien chose that moment to enter the foyer, his face changing from anger to shock as soon as he saw her face. He dismissed his doorman with a wave of his hand before walking outside to Tessa.

'Tess... I... what? What happened to ye-'

'You happened. Your stupid games did this, I hope you are finally happy with your little revenge.' Tessa spat each word, revelling in the despair marring Damien's face. He began to shake his head emphatically.

\'No, n-no, no, no... this wasn't... it can't be. W-what happenin'? How 'n that happen?' While he stumbled over his words, Tessa rolled up her sleeves to show all of the bruises present there, and pulled up her shirt to reveal the deep blush of purple over her cracked ribs.

'This? Yes, this is where your attack puppy stomped my face and smashed my nose. This is where he put the boot to my ribs and dragged me across the floor. Did you know that he threatened to rape me? That was pleasant. You did this, you put that sick... thing onto my trail. Hel, you tried to have me killed. Do you know what the punishment is for someone who kills an Agent?' She said furiously, pointing out each of her nasty bruises for emphasis as she spoke. Damien began to look ill.

'No! No! 'Is ain't right. 'Is ain't how'n it s'posed ter be. Tessie... I nev'r mean fer dat.' Tessa flinched when Damien used his usual pet name for her but shrugged it off.

'Well you should have thought of that before you paid someone to unleash that monster,' she responded as way of goodbye, turning on her heel to leave. While she didn't feel a lot better, getting all of that off her chest had certainly helped.

'Tessie, wait!' Called Damien after her, but it was too late. She was already across the market, the dust flying in her wake. She left him gaping in his guilt and confusion.

Tessa returned to the healing centre feeling oddly victorious. She bounced into Lee's room and settled at her usual spot by his side. He was improving by leaps and bounds, having started murmuring in his sleep and almost reaching consciousness. Tessa fell asleep again at his side, exhausted but calmed after her confrontation. She slept fitfully, strange and often terrifying dreams disturbing her. When she awoke, she found that Lee had draped an arm around her shoulders. Tessa jerked up when she realised that he must have moved at some point, and sure enough, he was gazing back at her. Her heart leapt as they smiled at each other, just sharing a look and happiness in the knowledge that the other was alive. Tessa moved up onto the bed beside Lee, curling up into his arms. They fell asleep in that embrace, finally resting easily.

Chapter Eighteen

T essa had begun to get a newfound appreciation and disgust for daytime television thanks to her time at the healing centre. The endless supply of trash was excellent for whiling away the hours, but there was only so much she could handle. She channel surfed idly, waiting for Lee to be done with his latest array of tests. The reddened face of a local politician filled the screen as she flipped to a 24/7 news channel, making Tessa gag dramatically. She was about to flip over when she caught what he was saying.

'It is for this reason that my party and I have put forward a bill regarding the clear identification and segregation of all non-humans, these so called magickal peoples. It is a matter of safety that these predators are removed from our population.' He raved as the camera swung back to the reporter. The juxtaposition of the red-faced, bland man in a worsted grey suit to the svelte news reporter with perfectly coiffed hair was telling.

'You are very vocal on the matter Mr Parsons. Do you really think you will pass this bill given that it will ostracise many of your voters?' Came a question from behind a microphone. The obese, balding, putrescent man nodded more emphatically than Tessa thought possible.

'Yes! Given recent events, I think this is finally a time for humans to band together and eradicate this problem. In the past violent witch hunts have not worked, but in a modern era of political power, we finally have a chance. There is no space for non-humans in our beautiful region. I believe this will pave the way for many other governments, perhaps finally becoming an international issue.'

'But don't you fear this will incite violence?' Another reporter, more coiffed hair and power suited feminine nature.

'Perhaps it shall, but perhaps it is needed to finally free ourselves from this scourge.' Mr Parsons looked directly down the barrel of the camera, his dark eyes full of malice and loathing. Tessa flicked off the TV sadly, the image of his glare burnt into her retinas.

If this zealot got his wish, it would be a very bad time to be a witch. Tessa pondered the timing, there had been so many murders, both mundane and magickal alike, so why was this being raised now? There had always been murmurings of this general idea, but this was the first big, public push.

Tessa was terrified at the idea that this may succeed, that all of magick kind would be ostracised and criminalised. It was this fear, this deep-rooted phobia of hers that had finally come to life and now spurred her into action. The safe and soothing blue walls of the hospital had become bland, sitting and healing had lost its appeal, even waiting for Lee seemed less important now she knew he was safe.

Tessa wrenched herself out of bed, got dressed and wrote Lee a note. The fuzzy haired asshole had to have a bolt hole somewhere in North Bayton, so she would start with that warehouse. She also called in to the office and requested a list of employees for that warehouse district, along with identification photos. He had to live or work in the area, given how well he seemed to know the laneways and hidey holes. A rat never strays far from its nest. She was ready to hit the streets.

Chapter Nineteen

As she creaked open the warehouse door, Tessa was hit by the memories leading up to her kidnapping. She had to physically shake her head to clear it before she could carry on and step into the huge space. Luckily the building was apparently normally used mainly for storage, so she didn't have employees watching her poke around. When she had called the company who owned it, she was also told it had recently been cleared in order for a new shipment to arrive, due in the next week or so.

Finally, she was getting a break, less clutter meant less to search. She went over every inch of the internal space, even kicking a few stray newspapers aside in case some hidey hole was below them. When she found nothing on the floor and walls, Tessa finally looked up.

'You have got to be shitting me.' There was a small array of scratch marks as well as dust free swipes along a beam running over a mezzanine area. The scratch marks, and rope like patterns in the dust... a grappling hook? Tessa scrunched her face up at the plausibility but sheer oddness of her finding. How had he gotten up there so fast? She had only been a few seconds behind him, but he had disappeared, and she was sure she hadn't seen a rope hanging down. While she thought about her current predicament, Tessa idly scratched her head, the tension running through her neck heralding an oncoming headache

'Well, onwards and upwards,' she resolved, plotting a path up to the dusty and cobwebbed mezzanine. After climbing the only ladder present, an ancient effort riddled with rust, Tessa carefully touched the toe of her boot to the mezzanine floor. It seemed sturdy enough, but she could never quite be sure. Certainly not sure enough to calm her overacting imagination, which was presenting her psyche with images involving a rusty break, a nasty fall and a whole lot of death.

Taking a deep breath, Tessa put most of her weight out onto the floor, then stepped fully off the ladder. It held, and she exhaled the breath in a thankful prayer. The second she grabbed the hand rail, a high screech of metal on oxidised metal rent the air and a shower of rust shards fell to the floor. Tessa felt ill and tore her hand away, swearing to not use it again. Step by step, she inched along until she reached the beam with the scuff marks and scratches. Reaching up, she carefully felt along it, finding that rather than being merely scratches, there were deep scores in the metal. Something had forced its way over the beam, and moved slightly.

'Ok... so a fluffy murderer with a super fast grappling hook? Who is killing based on a movie... seriously!' Tessa exclaimed, exhaling sharply in her frustration. It was all so implausible. Ahead lay more rusted mezzanine floor, cobwebs and dust, however they had been disturbed, and recently. Following the path along the walkway, Tessa came to a door. It was so coated in filth that it was impossible to see from the ground level. She gingerly tested the handle and was surprised when it easily clicked open. Even more surprising was the lack of noise when she pushed it open to reveal another walkway over another warehouse, this one with a good deal more items in it.

There was less dust, however there was just as much rust, and Tessa had to wrinkle her nose when she identified little piles of rat faeces. She visibly shuddered, more freaked out by the droppings than the height or ubiquitous dust. The shudder made the walkway creak ominously, another shower of rust fell along with the 'plink' of what was probably a screw. Tessa shuffled another step forward, her breath held tight in fear. Another step, nearly there.

Plink.

Another metallic screech filled the gloom before it settled back into deafening silence.

Plink.

The rusty floor beneath her shuddered violently, then dropped away. Tessa felt her world slow, she was suspended in midair, the mezzanine collapsing beneath her. A millisecond passed, then Tessa was falling too, instinctively curling herself around her precious organs. She struck a shelving unit, slamming into it before bouncing off and splaying onto the floor. The shelf took off a lot of momentum, the majority of the force spread along her side and caused her to land spread eagled on her back. The air was forced from her lungs, bursting forth in a vicious gasp. She stared up at the ceiling, fighting for air in futile desperation. Lucky to be alive, Tessa slowed her breathing and gradually brought herself back to normal. Sharp pain flooded her side with every inspiration, and she knew something was at least cracked, again.

Another pain throbbed beneath her, and Tessa rolled slightly to reach beneath her. One of the screws from the walkway, rusted and ugly. Tessa was about to throw it away when a glint caught her eye. It was scratched, someone had to have used a tool on it recently and in doing, scratched off the decay. Sitting up abruptly, Tessa scrabbled around the mouldy cardboard boxes to find the other screws. She could only find one other, and sure enough, it was similarly tampered with.

Sighing, she grabbed one of her little evidence baggies out and threw the screws in. Someone had booby trapped that walkway, and Tessa had wandered straight into it. She took some pictures of the debris and the collapsed walkway to add to fuzzy head's charges. At this point it was a death sentence anyway, but it didn't hurt to have some extra evidence.

Hitching herself up, she thrust the thoughts about someone trying to kill her out of her mind, solely focused on catching the bastard. An exploration of the second warehouse revealed plenty of exits into the surrounding area, all relatively well used. She had tracked him this far but could go no further. Blowing a stray lock of hair out of her face, Tessa sighed loudly, feeling a little stumped.

Glancing around the room one last time before she left revealed only boxes, shelving... and a constant red light!

A security camera was set high on the ceiling, barely noticeable if it wasn't for the little LED light breaking through the false dusk created by the warehouse itself. She had her next step, the last straw to be grasped.

Chapter Twenty

Back at the hospital, Tessa called in to the other warehouse owners and had the CCTV camera footage sent over to her to view on her tablet. She had just started to scroll through it around the time of her attack when Lee began to rouse.

'Hello beautiful. Was worried I wouldn't see you again.' He murmured, voice husky from lack of use.

'Of course you were gonna see me. Can't get away that easily. You saved me... well you saved both of us... Thank you, I love you.' Tessa said to Lee, tripping over her words in an effort to to get out everything she had been thinking about the last few days. Lee nodded slowly and beckoned her closer so she could hear.

'I know.' He replied, earning a swat on the shoulder and a groan from Tessa for his efforts.

'I was trying to be serious!' Sulked Tessa, mostly in jest. She was regretting introducing him to Star Wars. He gently took her hand before pulling her onto the bed and enveloping her in his arms.

'Hey you are supposed to be resting! And healing!'

'I'm bored with resting.'

'You only just woke up!'

'Yes, and I am bored!' finished Lee, flinching as he hit his bruised face trying to nuzzle into her neck. It was at that moment that a young healer walked in and dropped her files in surprise and embarrassment. Tessa was now lying on top of Lee, arms and legs akimbo and his face buried into her neck. It must have looked a lot worse than it was. The healer covered her face, speaking through her hands.

'Oh! I am so sorry... I came to do checks and give you treatment... I can come back later.' Stuttered the poor girl, going very red under her hands. Tessa scrambled to get up, trying not to laugh at the girls position.

'Oh no, he was just being a ratbag, you can have him! I have some work to do and will come back later.' She turned to Lee before continuing. 'Now be good! You need to heal so we can finish this case. I will talk to you when I get back about everything.' Tessa leant down to kiss him gently on the head before leaving, giving the mortified healer a wide berth. Her own room had since been reassigned at her request, so Tessa settled in the pretty but functional visitors room. She wasn't willing to admit to the healers that she had injured herself anew, hoping that the medicines she was still taking would be enough.

Grabbing a drink from the ancient vending machine, she settled in again to start watching the security footage. Tessa slapped herself on the forehead when she realised that the video had been reset in transit and she would have to scan through it all again.

There was nothing out of the ordinary aside from the fact that an extraordinary amount of rats seemed to have set up home in the warehouse, as well as the occasional stray cat hunting for said rats. That explained all the mess. Tessa sighed and scrolled through further.

When a door cracked open and a head peeked in she scrambled to press the play button. The person entered, followed by another. Tessa raised an eyebrow when she realised that this was clearly some kind of clandestine meeting between the fuzzy haired killer and another man who had his back to the camera. She could see the killer's face clearly, framed by a halo of hair that glowed in the sunlight from the door. Tessa checked the time signature on the movie, four hours before her attack.

They weren't there long, but the conversation was clearly rather friendly. The other man was repeatedly touching the killers shoulder and nodding, leaning in to talk. Tessa quirked at his odd body language, so affectionate and fatherly. Could it be that someone was influencing fluffy to kill? The conversation wrapped up quickly, with the fatherly man turning to leave. She tapped the pause button when his face was revealed and zoomed in.

Her mouth went dry as recognition flared. Senator Parsons, in all his grotesque glory, was having a secret meeting with the Bayton Magickal Killer? Well, that made the urgency to pass these ridiculous magickal segregation make sense.

Tessa was willing to bet that Senator Parsons had set up this entire series of murderous events. Politicians always had left a bad taste in her mouth. She took a few incriminating screen caps and scrolled on further, pausing it again as an email marked urgent popped up. The Agency had come through again, with a list of warehouse employees, complete with employment pictures.

Some little paper pusher Sibyl deserved a raise, circled in red was one Patric Wills, the fluffy hate fuelled murderer himself.

Tessa mused a moment on how someone so fluffy could be so deadly before shaking her head at her own silliness. The last known address was listed, so after checking in with Lee she went to the Agency.

As all evidence pointed to a non-magickal affair, Tessa didn't bother with her usual magickal kit. Instead, she just grabbed some salt and perused the available array of weapons. A sucker for a classic, she chose her favourite blessed Colt 45, a newer Smith and Wesson, as well as a few clever little daggers which could be concealed about the body. Feeling a little overkill but much more secure, Tessa was ready to go.

On her way out Tessa dropped in to the office of Sir McAdams, greeting his harried secretary. She seemed to be disappearing under a mountain of papers, all of which appeared to be press communications. Her phone was ringing away, its glaring red light indicating calls had already been missed. Tessa swallowed hard, she was sure that all of this had to be about her case. Not only did the livelihoods and lives of her people depend on this, but also her beloved Agency.

Sir McAdams wasn't faring much better, his face even redder than usual. Worried he was going to pop a blood vessel; Tessa quickly gave him a run-down of where she was going and what she was going to do. The reply was clear.

'Don't be too gentle.'

Chapter Twenty-One

Patric Wills lived in a cheaper area of North Bayton, characterised by spindly trees and sparse patches of grass. The needles and drug bags were just slightly better hidden here. Clearly being a murderous warehouse employee was not a lucrative business. His house was a rotting Victorian carcass, long ago split into multiple residences to maximise income from the place. As much as Tessa loved the Victorian style, this dilapidated corpse was just depressing.

The main door was rotted through, and flagged on the breeze, having never been repaired after being bashed in. Inside the walls were thick with graffiti and grime, broken only by the occasional cockroach. Wills lived on the second floor, so Tessa navigated the stairs carefully, hopping over the ones someone had previously fallen through. A door slammed as soon as she reached the main hall, muffling the mewling of the owner's cat collection. Clearly the resident spy was satisfied and did not want to be seen. Tessa shook her head and continued until she found number 7, drawing her gun before rapping on it curtly.

A few seconds passed, the howling of the cats and the scritching of several large roaches were the only sounds breaking the musty silence. Taking her cue, Tessa kicked in the door, beyond caring about the damage. She could have lock picked it, but kicking the door in just made her feel better. It is not like there was much door left, nor resistance to her boot.

The inside of the apartment was much more squalid than the exterior, with rubbish littering the floor and every wall streaked with grime and stains of every shade of brown. The state of the place made her gag repeatedly, while the stench made her eyes water.

Picking her way through the slum, Tessa scoured the den for any kind of life. It bloomed on dirty plates or scuttled along the floors, however no human life seemed to be present. The DVD of *Denizens of Darkness* had pride of place in front of an ancient television, clearly something Patric had watched again and again.

A second, more thorough check confirmed that no one was home, however it did reveal a series of notebooks stashed under his mattress, along with his dreadful porn collection. Not willing to touch any more than she needed to, Tessa quickly dragged the books into the main room and dumped them on the table.

They were filled with scribble, long litanies on the evils of magick and its practitioners. Here and there were articles cut from newspapers and magazines, each spawning a new rant based on its 'evidence'.

She flicked through the remaining six books, but they were all the same. If anything, they were significantly worse. By the fifth book Patric had begun to write out elaborate fantasies of killing magickal beings, and by the sixth he had illustrated them. It seemed killing them wasn't enough, the goal was eradication of her people. It was then Tessa hit pay dirt. It seemed that "Mr Man" and "The Man With The Plan" had promised to eradicate magick kind if Patric helped. Here was written proof that someone else was involved, and Tessa was entirely sure this "Mr Man" was Senator Parsons. She was just patting herself on the back when a shout rang out from the hallway.

'What the *fuck*?'

The door flew open fully, pushed by a very angry Patric Wills. He was brandishing a knife which was already crusted with dried blood and dirt. Tessa hoped that the blood was old but wasn't convinced as it came flying at her. She dove to the side, trying not to think about what filth was now attached to her as she fell to the grimy carpet. The texture could only be described as crusty. Patric had fallen into a pile of rubbish, and was working hard to get out of it.

Tessa leapt to her feet, not even bothering to pull out her knife for this clumsy fool. The man himself had finally battled his way out of the trash and was now struggling to stand. When he was finally on his feet Tessa whistled loudly before talking.

'Hey asshole, I found your ratty little bolt hole. I finally get to take you in for putting back the magickal community by about 40 years. And being a murderous little bastard.' She managed to keep her voice even, despite her anger. This was the man who had made those women suffer so, who had inspired hate and violence to her people. To her surprise and intense ire, Patric merely smiled at Tessa.

'About time. Pretty weak for someone with all those unnatural powers your kind have. Don't you want to know why?' He asked, a mock coyness tainting his words.

'Not really, but I am sure you are going to tell me anyway. Why kill those women?' Tessa responded, matching his smirk.

'Who better to kill than the women, especially the young and beautiful ones. It's the best way to get people pissed off, aside from kids. But I couldn't kill kids you know?' As Patric spoke Tessa noticed lunacy glowing from his eyes.

'Well aren't you quite the modern saint?' she quipped with a roll of her eyes and a click of her tongue.

'Quite. I did this for the safety of all humans, to inspire the eradication of the freaks and make a safer world. If you had have just let me finish my work I would have saved more lives then I took. They were sacrifices in order to protect humanit...'

'Oh shut up you bigoted fool, I am sick of listening to your madness.' Interjected Tessa angrily. Unfortunately it just caused Patric to smile more.

'What are you going to do, cast a spell on me?' taunted Patric, making his voice a childish and petulant tone.

'No, this,' responded Tessa, balling her small hand into a fist and punching him right between the eyes. There was a satisfying crunch as the asshole dropped like a stone. He hit the floor heavily, cracking the ancient wooden floor boards.

Resisting the urge to really lay into him, Tessa pulled out her phone to call someone to collect her now unconscious murderer, before snapping on the Agency cuffs. Very slimline and made from silver reinforced with a myriad of blocking and binding spells, the cuffs were made for far greater game than a scrawny diabetic human, but they would hold Patric well enough.

Tessa used the wait time to have a bit more of a poke around. Nothing else really stood out to her, aside from a tiny scrap of paper hidden under the phone, scrawled with a mobile number and "The Man With The Plan." Tessa took note of the number in her phone, then placed the slip in a plastic baggie before setting it aside with the notebooks. She was willing to bet that the number was that of Senator Parsons, and he was indeed the man with the plan.

Trying to ignore the fetid nature of her surroundings, Tessa fidgeted impatiently while waiting for the cavalry to come galloping in. At one point Patrick started to rouse but a quick cuff to the head soon put him out again.

Tessa flinched as her stomach growled angrily, a gruff reminder that she had eaten very little and done too much. Rifling through the cupboards revealed that Patric had as good a taste in food as he had in decor. Most of it was well into rot, incubi for the fungal masses. That which was unspoiled was all of a greasy nature, and all with some variety of meat. Tessa decided to just grin and bear it.

She was blissfully happy when the unique Agency sirens began to wail in the distance, growing ever closer to the squat.

Soon after, heavy footsteps beat a firm tattoo up the stairs, then a simple, masculine knock rang out. Given that there was very little left of the door, Tessa thought that was very polite. She greeted Louis Fitzgibbons warmly. Louis was one of the few people in the Agency that Tessa could remotely tolerate, aside from a few techs and the interns she studied with. He had a warm open face and a dimpled smile, despite to horrors an Agent faced. A flash of shock crossed his demeanour as he noticed the bruising on Tessa's face, but he politely quashed it into a pleasant neutrality.

'This the fool starting up the witch hunts? Looks pretty pathetic, doesn't he?' asked Louis, a slight but unrecognisable foreign lilt marring his words. He never talked about his past, and Tessa never asked. They all had their little secrets, just like she was heir to the famous Bale family. Also, that her mother had tried to kill her.

'This is he, complete with a stack of evidence. Name is Patric Wills, but he didn't do this alone.' Louis raised an eyebrow to Tessa quizzically but said nothing. She sighed audibly and pulled a hand through her hair. 'Everything points to Senator Parsons putting him up to it. Patric was murderous and completely cock-a-doodle-doo, but I don't think he would have gotten organised enough to do anything about this without the aid from the illustrious Senator.'

Nodding as she spoke, Louis agreed while beginning to look very unhappy.

'Good luck to that, not much shit sticks to that asshole. Not the first time I heard his name in connection to something disgusting.' With that he stomped over to the still unconscious Patric, scooped him up with very little grace and dragged him out the door.

Tessa picked up the books and the number before locking off the door. The forensic crew would come through later to try to find anything else. As she stepped out the front door Tessa still felt the darkness and grime from that house clinging to every inch of her body. It was a feeling that would last a very long time.

Chapter Twenty-Two

Weeks passed, and sure enough, Senator Parsons evaded every charge they could throw at him. The general hatred for all things occult dissipated rapidly when the public realised that the murderer was one of their own. Interestingly enough, the public then turned on Patric Wills, protests and calls for his death began to resonate around the city.

The Agency lost its final bid to make Senator Parsons answerable for crimes, much to Tessa' grave disappointment. Lee was eventually released from the healers with a good enough patch up job that he could return to work. Sir McAdams finally revealed the pawn he had played to save Tessa, drafting Lee as a professional hunter and back up to Tessa. She almost hugged Sir McAdams, until a suggestive leer practically undressed her on the spot and she stopped short.

Everything seemed rather neatly tied off, but one part still niggled at Tessa. The fact that Senator Parsons had almost wrangled a complete genocide and had gotten off scot-free was a thorn in her side. She stayed up late one night with Lee, hatching a plan.

Her hair shortened and temporarily dyed blonde, Tessa finished the final touches on her make up. She could barely recognise herself with a more natural tone, none of her usual dark eyes and cherry red lips. This look was all glitter and nude tones, the kind of make-up favoured by the trendier sex workers these days. A tight mini skirt along with a strappy top and a push up bra completed the look. Lee had almost spat his morning coffee when he saw Tessa, declaring that the look was a shocking waste of her looks. She took this as a sign as it was complete.

Strapping on her glittery gold heels and grabbing a clutch purse as the taxi tooted out the front, Tessa nodded to Lee, who would leave shortly after. He would take her car over, just to make sure they were separated from the main event.

The ride over to the offices of Senator Parsons was short and sweet, especially given that the taxi driver used every corner as an attempt to look up Tessa's skirt. She breezed into the offices, turning a few heads as she went and draped herself over the usefully placed chest-high bench in front of the receptionist.

'Hi, I'm Cara, the Senator has an, uh, appointment.' Breathed Tessa suggestively. Clearly the receptionist was unimpressed and simply snorted and jabbed her thumb towards a door over her shoulder. Tessa stepped through the metal detectors confidently, she didn't need any weapons for this take-down. Sticking her butt out as far as possible as she sashayed into the office, Tessa quickly shut the door before Senator Parsons exclamation of 'What the fuck?' could be heard. Tessa moved quickly, placing herself in front of him before he could rise out of his chair.

'What the... who the fuck are... YOU, you're that fucking witch bitch who dragged me through the courts with your bullshit!' he spluttered. Tessa spread her legs a little in order to lean down and meet him face to face.

'Aww you remember me, I'm touched. Now-now, is that any way for a fine, upstanding Senator such as yourself to talk?' she asked, hitting a few seductive poses as she leant on the desk a little, revealing even more cleavage.

'Like I give a shit what some whore of Hel thinks,' spat back the senator. Tessa turned around and put her butt on the edge of the desk before throwing her head back and laughing.

'My my, glad to see that nothing has changed, you are still the ignorant bigot you always were. Well...' Tessa took a moment to walk around the desk and spun the senator around in his chair. This way, he faced the enormous window overlooking the city. She dipped her head low and took a short pause before looking into his squinty little piggy eyes. 'Here is the thing senator, see this huge city of people? There is far more magickal people in this city than you can even fathom, and even more of the non-humanoid kind. I am sure we will all be keeping a real close eye on you, cowboy. Might not want to go too far off the reservation there boy."

'I don't respond to threats made by abominations, aberrations of humankind'

Tessa grinned widely, leaning in close to whisper in his ear. She was pretty sure the window got a good eyeful of what was up her skirt. She had purposely worn very little in the way of underwear.

'Oh senator, I was merely stating facts. I was even being helpful if you must. Not everyone takes as kindly to genocide as I do,' she finished, flouncing over to the small bar to pour herself a drink. Walking back to view the senator once more, Tessa raised her glass to him, downed the contents and stalked out. She hopped back into the waiting taxi, quickly changing into the spare clothes she had left in there. The cabbie's day had clearly been made, and he thanked her profusely as she paid him outside the diner she had agreed to meet Lee at.

A cliché bell chimed as she stepped in, throwing her sexy bait clothes in the bin on the way through. Lee sat at their favourite table, as unruffled as ever, and Tessa slid into the spot beside him.

'Well, how did they turn out?' she asked, using a napkin to wipe off the glittery make-up.

'Absolutely perfect. You should be an actress my dear! We got perfect, high-resolution shots, all in very compromising positions. We just need to mix up the order a little and make some prints for the media, his opposition and his wife.' They both grinned from ear to ear, overjoyed at their success. 'C'mon Helcat, let's get you home and get rid of that godawful hair colour,' continued Lee, scooting Tessa out of the booth. She kissed him long and hard before they walked out hand in hand.

Epilogue

Tessa eventually managed to return the engagement rings to Susan after handing in her final reports. Now there was no obsidian horned demon to abduct and rudely interrupt her, no murders to ruin her day, she could organise a discreet coffee date with Susan. Despite the many delays the girl still seemed happy to see her.

'Lady Bale, I am so glad to see you!' A young girl with a shock of blue hair pouffed up on top of her head and an all plaid outfit bounded over to the table Tessa had organised to meet at. This is exactly who she had envisioned marrying the very gothic Missy Peirce.

'Hello Susan, glad to see you! These are some unique rings.' Tessa said by way of greeting as she handed over the black velvet pouch that contained the rings. Pouncing cats forming the shank and a blood red ruby certainly stood out but seemed to mean something to the girls. Tessa had an internal laugh, calling them girls when they were barely a year younger than herself. She couldn't help but feel an age gap, or at least a maturity gap.

'Look at them. I can't believe I managed to buy something so pretty for my love. I hope she says yes. Do you think she will say yes?' Now Susan was starting to cry, running the full gamut of emotions in a single minute. Tessa nodded emphatically. Of their love she had no doubt, but she was unsure about their youth. Still, it wasn't up to her to be a dream killer, she just wanted to deliver the rings and get out of there. 'Thanks miss. I'm gonna invite you to the wedding if you want. I promise.'

'Sure thing.' *Just don't call me if she says no*, Tessa added to herself.

For a sneak peek into the third book in the Bayton Agency series, keep reading... This is Demon Enchanted.

Chapter One

'**L**ady Contessa, DUCK!'

This was always the problem with new transfers, it took so long to break them out of using her full name. Tessa shook her head as she swerved a king-hit from a spirit possessed accountant, who had turned from mild mannered geek into a swinging, hissing and spitting hellion overnight. When his family had been beaten to the brink of death, they finally called the Agency in. This would be a simple tear 'em free exorcism, but they had to subdue the creature first.

Another blow whistled past her ear as Tessa leapt away again, however this time she countered, kicking off her back foot and coming up under the accountants extended arm, a sharp blow to the jaw, and he was done. The momentum of her punch tipped him over, and he landed heavily on his own garage floor. Kneeling on his chest to pin him, Tessa motioned to Lee to bring over the restraints. All the while she was fighting, he had simply leant against the roller door, as calm as a lake on the surface. His shrewd eyes watched every motion, just in case she needed back up. He handed her the blessed cuffs, as the new transfer, Billy cheered from the sidelines.

He was so green he might as well have been a tree and had just transferred here from out of state. As much as she hated babysitting a newbie, even Tessa had to admit that any fresh meat was needed to boost the flagging numbers at the Bayton Agency. It was a necessary evil.

Once the ex-family man was safely cuffed and stowed, Tessa began to unpack all that she needed for an exorcism. She set up her travel sized fire dish while Lee kept a foot on the hapless accountant's back.

The spirit-possessed had a habit of trying to wander when it was exorcism time, and Tessa was hoping to return the accountant, one Dodd Martin, in relatively good order. Whether his family would forgive him was another matter. To the mundane folks it didn't really seem to matter whether or not it was a case of "the spirit did it".

Handfuls of rosemary and oregano went into the dish and were soon smouldering away happily while Tessa set a salt circle around the prone man, closing it only when Lee had hopped out. The circle was completed with a bind rune, so when the offending spirit was wrenched loose it couldn't just toddle off to find another victim. Tessa began her chant as she added myrrh and frankincense to the dish, which soon began to spark. Billy watched on intently, beginning to shuffle closer to hear her murmuring. Tessa didn't bother to glance up, needing her utmost focus to finish the exorcism successfully and return the man in one piece, minus the spirit.

Thin tendrils of ghostly energy were beginning to trail from the nose and mouth of their captive, wending their way almost to the ceiling. The air within the circle began to thicken with it, settling across the whole circle until it was almost an opaque tube. As Tessa was about to utter the final banishing words, the small pinch of sulphur waiting in her hands, all Hel broke loose.

Billy unexpectedly tripped onto the circle, having leant too far over to hear Tessa speak. Down he went, kicking up the salt border and falling onto the prone accountant. They both sprawled across the floor, and a whole second passed before the mist descended rapidly and disappeared. The accountant stumbled to his feet, groggily weaving back and forth as he rose watery eyes to Tessa.

'What happened to me? Why was I doing all those things to my family? I could see it, but I couldn't stop it at all. What happened to me?'

Fully aware that a violent spirit was on the loose, Tessa held her poker face, even as the man in front of her collapsed into tears. She hadn't finished the incantation. Possessive spirits were damn tricky, and this could be a ruse.

'You were possessed. Probably still are, so why don't you sit tight while I put another salt circle around you?' Tessa said, flinching slightly at how harsh she sounded. The man before her looked sad and scared, but he slowly nodded anyway. That made Tessa pause, and she looked over to Billy.

He lay with his face turned away from her, arms and legs twitching gently. It took Tessa a few seconds to realise that the movement was not twitching, it was laughter, which was soon resounding around the room.

'Well, ain't this a boon. I possess a pathetic, whiny accountant and end up with an Agent. This is going to be fun indeed!' laughed Billy, or more specifically, the spirit within him. Tessa cringed as she weighed up the options before her, as well as how much trouble she would be in for letting the transfer baby hunter get possessed.

Lee chose that moment to step in, darting towards Billy who was slowly getting up. Clearly the spirit was taking some time getting used to its new body, flailing and wobbling wildly as it rose. It seemed much more at home controlling a flimsy pencil pusher rather than a well-muscled intern Agent.

Lee was almost upon the student now, preparing to tackle him to the ground. Suddenly Billy shot out a hand, and Lee stopped mid step. One foot was even suspended in the air, but he was unable to move. The possessed hunter began to laugh maniacally now, throwing his head back in sheer mirth.

'Now this is a turn of events indeed! Telekinesis at that, nice and powerful. This takes me back.' With a flick of his hand, Billy sent Lee flying backwards through one of the plaster walls. Luckily there was no brick beyond it, and Lee simply fell to the floor two rooms over. He didn't get up. Tessa was thankful they built houses cheap in Bayton. Double brick would have meant a much longer recovery time.

Billy twisted his head back to Tessa, grinning from ear to ear. The effect was unnatural, more movement than a human neck was capable of. It was more like an owl, and the loud cracks were testament to the stress the spirit was placing on the body.

'I bet you didn't know that this poor sap could do that. I don't think even he did. But I knew, oh yes, I did. This suuuure takes me back.' While the spirit prattled on, Tessa had palmed her knife, using its tip to carve a small sigil into the wall behind her. She was engraving the symbol covertly behind her back and could only pray that she had inscribed it properly. Hopefully the home owners would fogive her, but given that a demon had already been thrown through a few walls, it was a drop in the ocean. This was going to be expensive for the Agency.

'You see, I was once a witch, with skills you pathetic hunters today can only dream of. But I followed the rules, and let those idiots take me. I could have killed them all, but instead held to the harm none idea. You know what it got me girl? I'll tell ye, it got me burnt on a stake! Me, in all my power, burnt by these pathetic creatures...' He continued rambling as Tessa focused intently, boring down with her magick, tapping into the veins of power running through the Earth below her. Drawing it up, Tessa filled herself with it, until her own magick had been eclipsed completely, and she had a line remaining to the earth. She then completed the sigil, feeling its power snap into place.

Billy was still droning on about the various evils inflicted upon him by the 'cattle', when Tessa stepped towards him. He threw up a hand, while looking utterly smug.

'Oh no little girl, don't make me throw you around. I would hate to ruin this lovely conversation just for a few careless steps.' Tessa grinned back at him, stepping over the accountant who had thrown himself on the floor whimpering as soon as Billy had first piped up.

A quick calculation and a wordless prayer later, Tessa threw herself at Billy. He swiped his hand to the side, but Tessa kept going. Pure momentum meant both of them ended up on the floor. Billy took a few seconds to reorientate himself, so Tessa made best of it, pinning him to the floor by sitting on his chest. He waved his hands frantically, but nothing happened. The spirit inhabiting Billy lost his temper. He kicked and spluttered, but Tessa held firm.

'Evil bitch! What did you do? I will destroy you for this indignity,' spluttered Billy, the unnatural soul within him lighting up his eyes with an odd shade of yellow. Tessa simply shrugged.

'You can try poppet, but I don't like your chances. I have bound the magick of everyone in this room. So, you can't play your little tricks.' Her attempt at bravado was clearly failing, with Billy beginning to laugh. Sweat began to roll down her face as Tessa held tightly onto the power she had borrowed from the Earth, as it threatened to break loose and destroy her along with the entire block.

'And? That is your plan? Did you forget, witch, that you need your magick to do the ritual to get me out? I will escape and kill you far before then, even if I must do it manually!' Scorn disfigured the young man's face as he spoke, but Tessa laughed in it loudly. That finally shook up the possessed boy.

'Tut-tut, an old witch forgetting the old ways? The rules don't apply if you have an active connection to the oldest of magick! Tapping into the Earth so to speak. That is enough to take you down and then some!'

'Impossible! To do that you would have to... no one can handle that!'

'Hah! You know not what you are facing *boy*. Now we both know that the ritual is simply to raise and direct the power, so all it will take is...' Tessa faded off as she focused intently, arrowing her borrowed power directly down and into the now blathering Billy. With quite an effort she tore the spirit from his flesh, taking care not to damage the real Billy as she went. A quick glance to Lee revealed a look of utter reverence on the now conscious demon's face.

To complete the task, Tessa began compressing the invading soul smaller and smaller. Finally, it stopped fighting her and meekly winked out of existence, leaving a deafening absence of noise in its wake. She had completely destroyed a spirit. It shouldn't even be possible, but she had just done it. Slumping forward weakly, Tessa began to shake uncontrollably, sweat rolling down her face in salty rivulets. The Earth magick leached rapidly out of her, draining into the ether. With its retreat, Tessa collapsed completely, falling face first onto the floor.

Also by Ysadora Sonderling

The Bayton Agency
Demon Desired
Demon Desired
Demon Hunted

Standalone
Heaven for a Predator